Shoreline of Infinity

Issue 19 Winter 2020/21

**Award-winning science fiction magazine
published in Scotland for the Universe.**

ISSN 2059-2590

ISBN 978-1-9993331-9-5

Shoreline of Infinity is available in digital and print editions.

Submissions of fiction, art, reviews, poetry, non-fiction are welcomed: visit the website to find out how to submit.

www.shorelineofinfinity.com

Publisher

Shoreline of Infinity Publications / The New Curiosity Shop

Edinburgh

Scotland

231120

Contents

Cover: Stephen Daly

**Shoreline of Infinity
Science Fiction Magazine
Editorial Team**

Co-founder, Editor-in-Chief, Editor:
Noel Chidwick

Co-founder, Art Director:
Mark Toner

Deputy Editor & Poetry Editor:
Russell Jones

Reviews Editor:
Samantha Dolan

Non-fiction Editor:
Pippa Goldschmidt

Copy editors:
Iain Maloney, Russell Jones, Pippa
Goldschmidt, Richard Ridgwell

Fiction Consultant:
Eric Brown

First Contact

www.shorelineofinfinity.com

contact@shorelineofinfinity.com

Twitter: @shoreinf

and on Facebook amd Instagram

Pull up a Log

"Politicians should read science fiction, not westerns and detective stories."

—Arthur C Clarke,
The Making of Kubrick's 2001 (1970)

It's been about a year since the new variant coronavirus started to make itself known on planet Earth and, here on the Shoreline, it has been an especially surreal time. Here we publish stories that speculate on what might be and our writers have indeed speculated about global pandemics and other apocalyptic situations.

It makes you wonder that, if the Prime Minister and his colleagues had been regular readers of our publication or any of the world's great science fiction presses, maybe they would have acted sooner and more effectively to head off this threat before it became the national emergency that it did. Of the world leaders who have seemed to get some control of this situation in their own nations, I wonder how many are readers of science fiction, or have paid some attention to the blockbuster movies that have also carried this message of speculation on the precarious position of humanity on our planet.

Maybe this will have been a wake up call and more attention will be paid to what might be in our future planning from here on. We still have the global climate emergency awaiting our attention. Let's hope it will be more acceptable for our politicians to speculate on what might be when they meet for the UN Climate Change Conference in Glasgow next year and that good early decisions will be made.

So, enough doom and gloom, we have assembled a more cheery group of stories for you to enjoy in in this pandemic winter. Enjoy them. Keep safe. Keep everyone safe. Keep speculating and planning for a better tomorrow.

Mark Toner
Dumfries
November 2020

THE SILENT WOODS

Tony Ballantyne
and
Chris Beckett

Back in the autumn, after the forest gates were locked, Peter, as ever, had been part of the searches. The forest had been divided up into sections in the usual way, with a three-person team allocated to each, led either by a ministry scientist or a trained local like Peter himself. There'd been more than fifty teams from towns and villages all across the infected area. Peter had been with Roger Hardin, the Methodist minister, and Lenny Yarrow who ran the garage at Staunton. Their task had been to locate every single dead or dying tree in their designated patch, record its position, check its trunk for any suspicious lumps, and then search the ground beneath it with metal spikes.

The teams had kept in touch with walkie-talkies. For more than two hours, the word going back and forth between them had been that all the tested trees were clean. The searchers hadn't spoken of it to one another but secretly each one of them had begun to hope. Could it be possible that they'd finally got rid of the infestation, and this forest had gone back to just being an ordinary wood?

It had been just after midday when Peter found the first one. He'd slid his spike into the earth beneath a sickly-looking ash and felt the horribly familiar crunch.

"Here," he'd said quietly.

It was mid-December now. There were Christmas lights up on the High Street, and Jingle Bells playing in the shops, and everyone was wearing facemasks.

There were no Christmas trees, of course.

"So they're still out there, yeah?" asked Peter's daughter Rose over breakfast. She was only ten years old, but she was tall for her age, and confidently perceptive in a way that made her seem older than her years. Lately, she had become a little abrasive too, and Peter and his wife Judy had ruefully observed, though not without pride, that they seemed to be getting a stroppy teenager three years early.

"Afraid so," Peter said. "We found fourteen of them in the autumn searches."

"Perhaps that was all there were?"

"It's almost certain that we missed a few. We always do, it's a big forest and they aren't easy to find. But we *are* getting the numbers down and I'm sure if we just keep at it, a time will—"

"Maybe we should just cut down the forest," Judy said suddenly.

The tabloids called for the same every year, after all: *FOREST CHUMPS: Badgers or our kids? When will this PC madness end?*

Rose shook her head. "Miss Beswick says that we have to remember that there aren't many of them there now. Not like in the old days. And if they cut down the forest, what would happen to all the birds and foxes and minibeasts?"

"Quite right, Rose." Peter didn't agree with his daughter's teacher on many points, but she seemed to be following the approved line in this case. "The overall trend's a downwards one. We'll get there eventually. I really don't think cutting everything down is the answer."

"No," Judy said with a sigh. "Nor do I really. But you can't help thinking sometimes how lovely it would be to have a real Christmas again, without this threat hanging over us."

"But Christmas in a poisoned desert?"

"I know."

Judy turned to her daughter. "So you're keeping your facemask on all the time, aren't you, pet, and keeping away from the forest?"

Rose sighed. "Of course I am, Mum. I'm not a baby. And I've been made to go through the THINK list every autumn since I was pretty much *was* a baby." She began to recite in a sing-song voice: "*T is Take care near the forest. H is Help your friends by checking if they're acting strangely? I is for...*" She abandoned the song., "Come on Mum, the forest is all fenced off anyway, and now they've locked the gates."

"People always do find a way through," Peter said. "The human brain is pretty inventive when it's entirely focussed on a single objective and, once the creature's got itself established in your head, finding your way out there really is the only thing it cares about."

After Peter found that first one, all three men had laid down their spikes without a word, picked up their spades and begun to dig, their breath making cloudy puffs in the autumn air. Flinging aside shovelfuls of the dark earth that lay beneath the leaf mould, they'd unearthed three of them, three lumps of eyeless, headless, jelly-like flesh wedged end to end in a narrow tunnel. Mindworms. There were no eyes, no limbs, no brain, but they did have something resembling teeth. Horrible, sharp little triangles.

7

Lenny had radioed the other teams to tell them the bad news. Roger had fished out the bones for analysis. (Badger, they thought, but the ministry scientists would know for sure.) Peter, ministry trained at his own insistence way back when most people were still denying there was a problem, had put on gloves and a facemask and slit the first one open. It had a rank sweet smell and oozed a syrupy fluid. The spore sac was still intact, as expected at this time of year. It would have been ripe in six weeks or so if it had been left, ready for the worm to carry it up to the top of the tree around Christmastime, the one single journey of its mindless, meaningless life. After ten months lying fatly beneath the roots of a tree, slowly poisoning it as they digested their one meal, the mindworms moved up the trunk like maggots, in a series of telescoping peristaltic movements, but so slowly that they'd often been mistaken for fungal growths. When they were high enough, they simply split apart, releasing their spores to the wind.

Peter had removed the sacs carefully and placed each into one of the special bags that the ministry provided, sealing them up in the approved manner and then placing them into the designated metal container, which had a screw cap. As he tightened the lid, he'd realised he'd been holding his breath all that time.

"You know what, Roger," Peter said as they trudged on. "I respect your beliefs and all that, but I can't for the life of me see how you can believe in a benign God in a world where mindworms exist. Such horror, such utter horror, and yet it serves no purpose. Even the worm itself gets no pleasure from it."

But the radio had crackled before Roger had time to answer. A team working near Drybrook, two or three miles off, had found another mindworm, an early climber, already two metres up its tree. Half an hour later, while Peter and the others were testing the roots of a moribund beech, the team at Huntley had announced they'd found one too. Hope died then, as it did every year, one radio call at a time. That horrid realisation throughout the forest, that the worms were still here and that, however hard you tried to find each one, somewhere there'd always be an apparently innocuous blob that no one had noticed, slowly insinuating itself upwards.

Trudging back to their parked cars as darkness fell, Peter, Roger and Lenny had passed the hollow of a collapsed mineshaft, now choked up with ivy and old man's beard.

"Remember when your mum and dad used to warn you about the mines," Lenny had said. "It was the worst that could happen round here back then, wasn't it? Seems so innocent now."

"There was that girl last year," Peter said to his daughter over the breakfast table. "That fifteen-year-old who slept with that forestry worker to get the—"

"Alright, Peter," Judy interrupted him, with a warning look. "No need to go into details."

No, of course not, thought Peter. That had been dumb of him. Apart from anything else, every stratagem that Rose learned about was another one waiting there in her brain if a spore were ever to lodge there.

But then again, who were they kidding? Rose would have heard the story anyway. Whatever they were told or not told by adults, kids repeated these stories to each other all the time: real ones and made-up ones, suitably embellished with gore.

"I'd know if it was happening to me," said Rose. "I write how I feel in my diary. I look at it each night and ask myself if I feel the same as I did yesterday."

"That wouldn't necessarily work," said Judy, and Peter could hear her trying to suppress the anxiety in her voice. "You change from day to day anyway. We all do. And anyway, if the thing had got into your brain during the day, you wouldn't even care that you'd changed by the time you looked at your diary that night."

Peter observed his daughter with narrowed eyes. She hated the annual hysteria of the Christmas period. She hated the indignity of the town's collective fear. "The risk to any one individual isn't very great, Rose darling," he said, reaching across the table to touch her hand, "and you're quite right to refuse to get worked up about it. Good for you! I really mean that! I love that about you!

But the key thing to remember is that, if you ever find yourself thinking, even for a moment—"

"—about sneaking out into the forest, I must always tell you or mum or a teacher straightaway. I *know* Dad! *N is for Never hide it if you find yourself wanting to do funny things.* You tell me the same thing every winter, so do my teachers, so does the telly, so do the posters all over town."

"I'm sorry, love," said Judy. "We know you get bored of it, but we love you so much and we only keep drumming it into you because—"

"I know."

"You only have insight for a very short time," Peter said, "that's the thing. Your mum's quite right. An hour or two at most, and after that the mycelia have so thoroughly taken over your brain that the only thing driving you is the compulsion to deliver yourself up. And then—"

"—and then you don't tell anyone anything. I know. I've known that since I was three. I'd better go now. I need to get ready for school." She paused at the door, a knowing smile on her face. "All I'd need is a set of wire cutters, I suppose."

And suddenly Peter snapped. "Dammit, Rose! It isn't funny! This isn't some kind of joke!"

Rose flared up instantly as well. "I know it's not, Dad. They ate a girl in my school last year, remember? They ate Ursula. As everyone *constantly* reminds us."

Slamming the door behind her, she stomped upstairs to pack her satchel.

A few minutes earlier, Judy had been the one who was anxious, Peter the voice of reason. Now it was the other way round. Judy put her hand over his.

"Steady, love. She's not Libby."

He swallowed. Of *course* she wasn't Libby. But he remembered that Judy was trying to help, and forced himself to speak calmly.

"Should I go after her, do you think?"

"We'll speak to her when she comes down," Judy said. "She'll be alright: that's what we've got to remember. Like you always say, so long as she wears a facemask outside, the risk is pretty tiny, and she's got her head screwed on, our Rose. She really has."

"I know."

"You've put in a huge amount of work on reducing the risk in this town, more than anyone else. The searches, the committee, your work. I know that. Rose knows that. All our friends know it. We're very proud of you."

"But the thing people don't get is that it isn't like rabies or something. The thing is, people are still convinced they'll realise when it happens to them. How can they still think like that? They've seen others keep all their faculties, their charm, how they can still wheedle and reason. But it's like everyone thinks they're special, that they can stop the mindworm taking over at the core. And it's—"

He broke off, too close to tears to be able to continue. Judy stroked his hand. "I know," she said. "I know."

He nodded, not trusting himself to speak. He'd been fifteen. He was supposed to look after his little sister, but at five years old Libby had worked out how to distract her parents long enough to be able to run away. All on her own, she'd gone into the woods – there were no fences then – found an appropriate tree, dug her own tunnel with her bare hands, and crawled into it, there to be slowly eaten alive from the inside until all that was left of her was the brainless, nerveless lump of greyish jelly that had built itself out of her flesh, lazing at ease among her bones.

Peter had blamed himself ever since. But what could he have done? Mindworms were in a way the ultimate predator: predators that made their prey do all the work.

Suddenly Judy stopped stroking his hand. "Do we *have* any wire cutters?" she asked.

"Yes we do. Haven't used them for years, but they're in the shed."

"Lock it and hide the key."

"Don't worry. It is locked. I always keep it locked."

Rose put her head round the door. She wore a black and white scarf and a hat with the eyes and ears of a panda. "I'm going," she said.

"Do I not get a kiss?" asked Judy.

Rose shuffled into the room, proffering her cheek to her mother with a teenager's studied lack of enthusiasm.

"Me too," said Peter. He smelt chocolate on his daughter's breath. Her advent calendar.

"Bye," she said, pulling down her facemask and stepping outside.

Peter drove down the High Street to his morning surgery. In spite of the Christmas lights it wasn't much of a high street these days, what with everyone in facemasks, the almost tangible fear and all the boarded-up shops making it look like a mouth full of rotten teeth. He and Judy had discussed moving away themselves, of course – it wasn't as if they didn't have marketable skills – but they were both children of the forest and stubbornly attached to the place. There was a certain sort of person who, from the safety of comfortable homes in the middle of cities far away, loudly proclaimed the need to protect the ancient woodlands. Peter and Judy liked to think that they were actually walking the walk.

Also, they'd spent a lot of money on a very nice house which would be worth almost nothing if they moved. People moved out of the forest. Nobody ever moved in.

You had to keep this in proportion, Peter and Judy's friends told one another. Yes, the mindworms claimed a few lives each year, but so did car accidents, and no one moved out of a place because of that.

But they all knew there was a flaw in this argument. Car crashes were tragic but they didn't eat constantly into your mind and your dreams. When this time of year came round, you didn't have to have inhaled a spore to become obsessed by the thought of the dark forest out there beyond the fences. *Everyone* was obsessed by it, everyone was afraid of it, and everyone seemed to bring their fears to the doctor.

"Shirley had a nightmare about a jungle last night," said a plump woman with short red hair. "She said there were wild animals chasing her."

Peter nodded and turned to the little girl. "In your dream did you *want* to go into the jungle?" he asked.

She squirmed shyly. "No."

He leaned forward to make himself smaller and less intimidating. "What *did* you want to do, Shirley?"

Shirley looked up at her mother. "Tell the doctor," her mother said.

"I wanted to come out of the jungle and come home."

"And did you run?"

"Yes."

"Into the jungle or out of it?"

She smiled for the first time, amused by the strange obtuseness of adults. "Out of it, of course!"

"I see." He turned to the mother. "And is that how she described it as soon as she woke up?"

"Yes, she did."

"She spoke of running away? You're sure of that?"

"Yes."

"I think we're alright then."

"You think? Can you guarantee that she's safe, Doctor?"

Of course he couldn't give that guarantee. He couldn't guarantee that any medical treatment was 100% safe either. But no one was interested in such nuances. As far as his patients were concerned, his job was to tell them for certain that they were safe.

"I don't think you need to be worried," he told the mother, though he knew that this would be heard as the doctor saying there was no risk.

Peter gazed out of the window as he waited for the next patient. Two trees had once stood at the far side of the carpark, but they'd been cut down to open up an expanse of bare sky which currently showed the yellow tinge of winter. The town was full of tree stumps, and it seemed as if it was every week that he had to swerve around another felled tree on the way to work. Pointless acts of vandalism: the mindworms only ever appeared in the forest.

The next patient was Jennifer, a surgery regular, gaunt and with eyes hollow with worry and sleeplessness.

"I keep thinking I want to go into the forest and dig a hole under a tree."

He glanced at her notes on the screen and saw that she'd seen his colleague about the same thing only a few days ago. "And how long has this been going on?"

"Ever since October."

"I don't think we need to worry then, Jennifer. The searches in October are unsettling for all of us, but even the earliest spores don't appear until much later than that."

"It was a funny summer, Doctor. The leaves were falling early this year. The seasons are all over the place. How can you be sure about the spores?"

"I'm one of the searchers, Jennifer. I saw the worms myself, and I can assure you that none of the spore sacs would have been ripe until mid-November."

Again, though, he couldn't *really* be sure. He could only speak about the worms that had been found. But there was simply no time to explain all that to people, and no one was interested in explanations anyway.

Next it was another child, a little empty-eyed waif of a nine-year-old called Billy, accompanied by his granny. Peter knew that the mother, Pauline, was a heroin user, often too preoccupied with her habit to be available to Billy at all. The boy had been in care several times, but now the grandmother, Pauline's mother, had moved to the area. Lately, with a little input from children's social care, a more or less workable arrangement had been established in which mother and granny shared his care between them.

"How's my old mate Billy doing?" Peter's heart ached for the child. Mrs Tarton, the granny, made sure he was fed and clothed and taken to school, but she struck him as a cold woman, acting not out of love, and not even exactly out of duty, but out of a powerful need to prove herself better than her daughter, better than the people she imagined were judging her. She cared for him, but she didn't really care *about* him, so it seemed to Peter, and that meant that there was no one in the world, and never had been, to whom Billy was a delight in the way that Rose was a delight to himself and Judy.

Billy regarded Peter with opaque grey eyes. "Alright," he said.

"So what can I do for you?"

His granny answered for the child. She never seemed to give him time to speak. "He was with his mum last night. You know where they live, don't you, Doctor? Their garden backs onto the forest."

Peter knew exactly where they lived. Forty years ago the Woodside estate had been a very desirable location. Now it was where the council put the problem tenants, the ones who really didn't have any choice if they wanted a roof over their heads.

"Well, he was digging down there this morning when I came to pick him up," she said. "I had to wash the mud off his hands." She was bristling with self-righteousness. "They say in those leaflets that you've got to bring kids in for checking if they ever try digging near the fence, so I did, seeing as his mother certainly wasn't going to bother."

"I see. So what were you digging for, Billy?"

The boy refused to meet his eyes and would not answer. Peter felt his anxiety rising.

"I had a look," his granny said. "It's a big hole. His mum hadn't even noticed. He'd made a kind of lid out of sticks and turf to cover it up with."

Peter sighed. It was obviously a good thing if a mindworm infection could be detected before a child disappeared, but the treatment wasn't easy even so. It went on for months, was painful and debilitating, and could result in long-term impairments. This poor kid had had more than his share of trouble already.

"Did he tell you what he dug it for?" Peter asked.

"He wouldn't say, but there was money down there. I think it was the money his granddad gave him last week. I wondered if he was hiding it from his mum, a.k.a. my completely useless daughter. You know what these junkies are like. That girl nicks any money she can find for smack. Even from her own kid."

Knowing Pauline, this seemed like a very plausible explanation to Peter and he relaxed somewhat. Then it struck him how sad it was that news like this could have made him feel *better*. He leaned towards the boy.

"*Do* you have to hide your money from your mum, Billy?"

The boy hesitated. Finally he gave a tiny nod. "And my toys."

"Toys?" Peter tried to avoid sounding shocked, and held up a warning hand to tell Mrs Tarton not to answer on his behalf. "Does your mum sell your toys, then?"

Again, after a second's hesitation, a tiny nod. "She has to," Billy said in a small voice, exonerating his mother from blame or reproach in a way that Peter found heartbreaking, as if the child had simply accepted that she had no choice but to prioritise her habit over his needs.

Peter nodded. "Thank you, Billy, I appreciate you sharing that with me. Do you ever want to go out in the forest?"

The boy gave an incredulous snort. "Of course I fucking don't! There are fucking monsters out there!"

He stared at Peter as he swore. He was aiming to shock. *What are you going to do about it?*

"Language, Billy," his granny scolded. "You're not with your mother now. I'm sorry, Doctor, he doesn't hear it from us, but that woman has a mouth like a sewer."

"Don't worry about that. Now listen, Mrs Tarton. You did the right thing to bring him in, but—"

"Someone's got to do the right thing. The council says that's what we have to do, so I did it. His mum doesn't even bother making him wear a mask."

"I'm very sorry to hear that. But I don't think we're dealing with mindworms here."

He'd stopped worrying from the point that he heard about the money. It rang so true with what he knew of the family. It was a situation he'd seen so many times in the past.

"Are you sure?"

"Sure as I can be."

"So not completely sure." She paused, making her point. "Are you going to get him tested at the hospital?"

Her strident tone grated. He didn't hear concern for Billy, he heard a need to demonstrate that no one looked after the boy better than she did. "Mrs Tarton, we really can't have every child tested just in case, or we'd be testing all of them every day. That's just not possible. The resources just aren't there. And the disruption to children's lives would be too great in any case."

The grandmother wasn't impressed. "Is that what you'd say if he was some posh person's kid? Only I've heard that—"

Peter wasn't having that. "I'd say exactly the same thing."

She snorted. "Half of them go away on skiing trips till the spore season's over, from what I've heard. It's alright for some. All this talk about how we're all in it together and then they—"

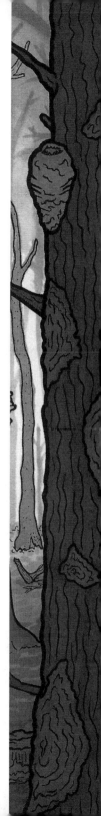

"Well, I'm here, Mrs Tarton," he told her, a little more sharply than he'd intended. "I'm always here this time of year, as I think you know. I'm always here. And I'm telling you I don't think we need worry about Billy. But do keep an eye on him, and when you or your husband take him back to his mum, have a good check on that hole he's dug and make sure that it doesn't go further than you thought. Any worries, come straight back to me."

"Oh I will," said Mrs Tarton in darkly meaningful tones. "I'll come straight back, you can be sure of that."

Peter rubbed his face with both hands as she shepherded Billy from the room. Peter's job, as far as his patients were concerned, was to come to absolutely definite judgements and to take responsibility for those judgements, so that they wouldn't have to. It was an impossible assignment. And yet he accepted the burden as his due, as if it were part of some kind of Sisyphean penance.

He shook his head, as if to clear it, and then leaned forward and called for the next patient. It was another mother with another child.

He was out on his rounds that afternoon when the police called to tell him that Billy had gone missing after school. He'd been supposed to go back to his granny's, but hadn't appeared.

"We went round his mum's, obviously," the officer said. "His mum was off her face upstairs, but there was a tunnel in the back garden going under the fence. So it looks to me like a mindworm case but I wanted to check with you, because his granny says you saw him this morning and told her it definitely wasn't."

The policeman didn't really want to 'check' anything, Peter knew. He wanted to let Peter know that he'd blundered and that his blunder had been noticed and logged. It would make no difference to the world if Peter explained that he'd never said he was definite. Definite was what everyone heard, and it was part of his penance that it was so.

"Okay. This clearly *is* a mindworm case," Peter said. "We need to get the forest search team out there right now. I'll fetch my torch and I'll be right there."

What a fool he'd been! What an unforgivable idiot! Once infected, the human mind, driven by this one implacable force, was infinitely devious and extraordinarily inventive. Victims *always* had a plausible story, for God's sake. Kids were taught that at school from the age of five. *Know what to expect* was the K in THINK: *Know what to expect, and expect clever tricks.* Peter himself had drummed it into Rose over and over. How could he have been such an idiot to have allowed himself to be fooled by the money and toy thing? It had been such an *obvious* ruse. Billy knew what the professionals thought about his mum. He knew what it was they pitied about him.

Judy and Rose weren't back yet when he arrived home. He scribbled a note, rummaged in the drawer in the hallway for the shed key hidden between the pages of an old address book, then hastily tugged on his boots and a warm coat, and went to fetch his torch.

Ought to hide those wire cutters, he thought, noticing them lying there as he left the shed and headed for the forest. There was no time now, though. The chances of finding Billy were fading with every minute that passed.

Stepping into the forest was stepping into another world. The silence, the sense of isolation. The world seemed dead at this time of year, the trees black and skeletal. The last shrivelled leaves that hung from the branches had died in place, and rattled at his passing.

No sign of the other searchers. He checked his phone. No messages.

He felt a surge of anger and anxiety. Anger that another child had gone missing and the authorities didn't seem to be taking it seriously, and anxiety for the child. Poor Billy, out there somewhere, heading deeper into the forest, making himself harder to locate. And the shadows were spreading as the sun was going down. In another hour it would be completely dark.

He moved forwards and backwards, unsure which way to go. And then, to his great surprise, he spotted, of all people, Susan

Ridgely, an old friend of Judy's. The fading light meant he couldn't quite see her, but surely that was her, about thirty yards away, standing beside a tree, waving across at him.

"He's right here!" she called out. "He says his best friend is under the tree. He says it's a dog called Furry."

Aha! That old trick! Just like Libby. Well, it wasn't going to work this time! Peter laughed with the relief of it.

"He doesn't have a dog," he called back as he ran towards her, already looking eagerly at the foot of the tree. "That's just how he's making sense of what his brain is telling him to do."

Because it always felt like something you longed for more than anything, didn't it? Kids weren't so devious back when it happened to his sister, back when no one really knew what was going on. They had no sense that this new drive inside them was something they'd have to conceal. And so, Libby had spoken quite openly about her best friend Boggles who lived in the forest and loved her very much. Until the day she disappeared, his parents had thought this was all rather sweet. They even played along with it: "So what's Boggles up to today, sweetheart? Do you think he's enjoying the sunny weather?" Peter had thought she was just trying to get more than her fair share of attention. He'd only paid attention to how the Boggles thing had made him feel, and not to what it might mean, and ever since he'd dragged his shame behind him like a ball and chain.

"Don't try and argue with him about it, Susan," he called. "I'll speak to him. I'll get him out."

He felt his heart lift. He would talk Billy out of the hole he'd got himself into. He'd climb down there with him if need be, he'd talk it over with him. Tell him about Libby and Boggles, hold him, bring him back again to the human world.

His phone pinged. It was a text message from Judy.

Peter, do you know where Rose is?

For God's sake, there was no time for that now. He hurriedly tapped out a reply.

Get back to you soon, Susan Ridgely has just found Billy.

He pushed the phone into his pocket as he hurried towards Susan. She was pointing to the spot where Billy was hiding.

He felt his phone vibrate. Impatiently, he held it to his ear. Judy's voice was shrill. "Susan isn't here!" she began. "She's in London with her mother!"

Peter cut her off as he got onto his hands and knees. Who cared where Susan was? What had that got to do with anything? He switched off the phone and started to claw at the leaves and soil.

"I'm coming Billy," he called. "I won't let it get you!"

Tony Ballantyne is the author of the Dream World, Penrose and Recursion novels as well as many acclaimed short stories that have appeared in magazines and anthologies around the world. He has been nominated for the BSFA and Philip K Dick awards. His latest book is Midway: literature, fantasy and science fiction come together in an original and very personal work

Chris Beckett is the author of eight novels and three short story collections. His novel, Dark Eden, was the winner of the Arthur C Clarke Award in 2012. His most recent novel, Two Tribes, came out in July 2020. Formerly a social worker and lecturer, he lives in Cambridge with his wife Maggie. .

We are Still Here

Anya Ow

The tourist screamed when they saw me, which was always hurtful. "You don't have a visa," I told them as I stayed partly submerged in the warm water. "Turn around."

They peered at me over the edge of their submersible. Shaped like a silver teardrop, the glass nose of a cockpit was boxed in by a holographic lattice that drew skeins of pattern-data over the tourist's pale face. Temperature and humidity in the red. Organic lifesigns nil. Radar and map distorted. As I drew closer, the tourist tried to hide their revulsion behind genteel fascination.

Art: Mark Toner

I was amused by their distaste. I could understand it – I could see myself reflected in the teardrop. Most of my natural-born skin was now heat-reflecting scale, my spine lengthened and fused with jointed bionics, legs folded and flattened into a sinuous tail. Once, one of the ethnic groups I could trace my ancestry to, called themselves the 'descendants of the dragon'. It may have amused them in turn to see how their children had evolved. Feathery red horns extended from the back of my skull through which I could breathe, the horns of a dragon made for a drowned world.

I waved. The tourist flinched. "My God," said the tourist as they checked their data, "the rumours were true. Singapore became a nation of semi-organic servitors."

"Turn around," I repeated.

"How many of you are there? This is amazing! By the way, your English is really good," the tourist said, beaming. "I'm Jeannie Langford. Call me Jeannie."

Frustrated, I closed my eyes and accessed shoalspace, projecting into the shared gestalt that interlinked every edited New Singaporean. "Hei this bodoh angmoh cmi lah. 'English veli good' my ass. Faster-faster process?"

"HQ say kenot shoot," said my handler-assistant, Lakshmi. "Wait world gahmen emo. Stand by ah. I checking."

Great. I looked back at Jeannie sourly. "You're within Singapore's sovereign waters. Leave," I said.

"Your city shows up on all readings as an empty ruin. There can't be many of you left that are even functional," Jeannie said, gesturing at the replanted walls of the building beside them.

New Singapore did look like a ruin to the untrained eye. Indigenous plants edited to withstand the humid heat crowned what had once been Terminal 1 of our acclaimed airport in a summer cloak of vines and ferns. Scarves of money plant climbers slung themselves in thick ropes between repurposed buildings and lamp posts, while beneath them crests of hyacinths crowned lushly tangled beds of water weeds. Insects drew slow circles through the rippling air. There were no birds.

"You're in our city. Leave," I said.

"You're a guardian for the city's remains, is that it? A resident AI or ASI? Your brain processor's very advanced. Unusual shape, too." Jeannie brought up a little mapped image of me on one of their holographic screens. "Incredible. You're nearly two centuries old on the scans. The tech we have would've rusted out in years."

"Wah lieu, it's 1819 all over again," I told Lakshmi. "Still kenot?"

"HQ say watch-see," Lakshmi said. Damn HQ. I slid into the water, ignoring Jeannie's call for me to stop. Swimming into the densely planted B2 level, I nestled myself within the water plants and waited.

Shoalspace was starting to focus on the intruder. They were rare in the equatorial band – the heat and humidity meant death within hours for anyone unedited and unprotected. "Who they think they is. Stamford Raffles 2.0?" "Sure got diseases." "Why kenot shoot?" "I thought angmoh all flee to Canada?" "Ira, be careful k?"

I defocused on the public peanut gallery pinging my mentions. Jeannie's submarine tried to follow me into B2, but soon resurfaced when the dense weeds reached for and threatened to choke its filters. They wrapped protectively around me in turn, obscuring me from sight and processing any pollutants that my scales had attracted from the surface air. The pod nosed around the submerged Terminal for an hour, occasionally stopping to sweep its surroundings with pale lines of blue light. To my annoyance, Jeannie then docked and emerged.

"Still kenot?" I pinged Lakshmi.

"Standby," Lakshmi said.

Curse the bureaucracy. "I know you're still there," Jeannie called out as they climbed out of the pod onto fern-choked escalators. "I don't mean you any harm, any of you. I just want to talk."

"HQ say go give a tour," Lakshmi said. They sounded doubtful. "Serious?"

"They want to kaypoh the pod." New technology did always make HQ curious, and I'd never seen anything as compact as the pod before. I bit down on my sigh and crept out of my makeshift lair with a flick of my tail, surfacing close to the escalator.

Jeannie smiled warmly as they noticed me. "There you are. I'm sorry if I startled you. What's your name?"

"Ira," I said.

"That's such a cool name!" Jeannie raised their palm and the silver bracelet over their wrist drew lines of blue light over my position. It was my turn to flinch. Oblivious, Jeannie studied the data as it was projected before their face on a screen. "You're 21% organic. That's truly fascinating. Even the most advanced organo-servitors I've seen were at best 11% organic. Maybe that's why you're so old."

"Are you a scientist?" I asked.

"In a way." Jeannie let out a little laugh. "No more universities out there to get degrees from. I'm more of a hedge-scientist."

New Singapore still had three universities, all of them free, one devoted to science. It figured that the rest of the world still thought education a luxury. "Why are you here?" I asked.

"I rigged up a program to NERZA – that's one of the world's last accessible, functional satellites – and used it to scan the equatorial belt for life signs," Jeannie said. They brought up a large map with a flick of their fingers. It was scarred maroon across the centre and over large blotches of a handful of other countries, wherever the world was now technically uninhabitable. Singapore showed up as a paler orange in a deep band of red.

"Hailat," Lakshmi said. Proof that the vast cooling plants under New Singapore and the bioengineering projects were working didn't feel good when it was displayed on someone else's map.

"Wow," I said, out of a lack of anything else I could think of to say. I willed HQ to shoot, eyeballing the autoturrets nestled in the ferns.

"That's right. The temperature's still deadly in this city, but it's somehow lower than the surrounding regions. Your creators must have hit on something truly innovative. That's why I'm here. To export Singapore's cooling technology to the world." Jeannie pointed at a spot near the southernmost tip of Australia. "This is where I'm from. We've been going through one bad fire season after another."

"Don't you have bionic tech?" I asked. Jeannie didn't look like they were in any hurry to leave the area and their pod.

"We do." Jeannie lifted one leg. "This baby's bionic. Lost it when I was young. Viral infection. Why?"

"You could use bionic tech to raise your optimal temperature," I said, hoping I wasn't giving away too much. "You won't need much cooling tech after that."

"People have tried that. It only works if you replace most of everything and heavily edit the rest on a cellular level," Jeannie said. They paused, their eyes widening. I grimaced as Jeannie flopped onto their knees and looked me over again. "Oh. You people...? *God.*"

"Thanks," I said, twitching my horns.

Jeannie blushed. "I didn't mean ... I've been so rude. I'm sorry. I really ... you do look like a cyborg. One of those Model-8 Alexans."

"Sure."

"That's what you people did? No offence. Edited your entire population into ..." Jeannie shivered. "I'd heard stories about your government during the 2100s, before Singapore went dark along with the rest of the equatorial belt, but this is ... it's hardly ethical."

I resisted the urge to fire some of my tail spikes in Jeannie's direction and forced a smile. "While the government's trying to decide what to do about you, I could give you a tour."

Jeannie beamed. "That's kind of you. I knew you'd see reason. Lead on."

I didn't like this part. I swam closer to the shore and hauled myself up. Valves whirred within my tail as the segments split down the centre into eight jointed sections, which allowed me to climb up onto the platform without sliding awkwardly. It also made me tower above Jeannie by a hand's breadth. The scales on my body arched to become tiny cooling fins in the soupy air.

Jeannie had taken several steps back. At my puzzled look, Jeannie said weakly, "I've never been fond of spiders."

"The number of legs is optional. I just find them more stable than just two. There's nothing wrong with spiders – we've preserved over half of our remaining native species. They're an important part of the ecosystem." I wished I didn't sound so defensive.

"I've offended you again. I'm sorry."

Jeannie didn't sound particularly contrite to me. I nodded anyway and made my way along the floor, taking care to give Jeannie a respectful berth. "This way."

"Where are we going?" Jeannie followed me, stopping every few steps to scan the area with their terminal.

"The Jewel. It should be more comfortable for you in there." It was also a bit of a walk from the Terminal. I could've swum the distance in a quarter of the time that it took us to traverse one of the Strands into the central dome of the old airport, the first of its kind in New Singapore.

Jeannie gasped as the air grew cooler the closer we walked, charged with the sound of a giant's constant inhalation. The Jewel drew breath through the massive waterfall in its heart, twice as vast as it had been when it had first been built. The percussion from the infinite veil of water shook its own microclimate through the dome, optimal for the banks of hydroponic tiers shelved around the waterfall in slow-moving intervals.

"It's so beautiful," Jeannie breathed. I inclined my head. "I've never seen anything like this. It looks so efficient. How do you people do it?"

"Our country's been preoccupied with the changing climate for centuries," I said. I gestured at the glass walls beyond the green tiers, which looked out to the pristine inland sea, a sea that had long swallowed all that we once were. "We didn't have a choice, as an island country."

"A very wealthy one, with an autocratic government," Jeannie said.

"Every government is imperfect. Some more than others." I tried to sound kinder than I felt. Everyone knew that the remaining governments that made up the World Government were fragile, venal things, still fighting over the remnants of the world that was. They did not see that change was irrevocable. That it did not have to be frightening. "We preferred to meet the challenge of survival head-on with all our resources rather than opt to retreat."

They looked at me with a strange expression. "Were you edited at birth? Into what you are now?"

"Everyone is."

"God, I can't even … I'm sorry, but. Doesn't anyone object?" Jeannie asked.

"Why?" The pity that Jeannie wore was hard to take. "My body lets me live here. In my home. Even after everyone else left island-countries like us to drown. When we weren't big enough or white enough to be given even a front-page obituary on world news platforms." I walked over to the vast waterfall, my sharpened feet clicking on the deck. The fruit trees were grown at careful intervals between the tiers. I pulled a starfruit from the closest and tossed it to Jeannie. "We'd always knew we'd have to adapt to thrive."

Jeannie examined the starfruit. They unsealed their helmet, which fed back into the folds of their clothes. Even in the Jewel they quickly began to sweat, but they took a bite of the starfruit and smiled. "It's sweet. I've never seen anything like this before. Not even in docudramas. Do you grow apples? Oranges?"

"Nothing that isn't indigenous to this area. We've learned our lessons."

"Lessons?" Jeannie asked. They tucked the fruit into their clothes and resealed their helmet. Their skin had reddened, turned shiny with sweat.

"The gene editing we used worked better with indigenous plants and fauna. Everything else either died quickly or caused side-effects. Diseases, mould, worse." I had been a child when the Red Spot leaf mange had burned through a quarter of our Jewels.

It had been the reason I had grown up knowing hunger. That was the last time we tried to grow strawberries.

"Could I walk around for a while in here? Take measurements?" Jeannie asked.

I waited. No objection from Lakshmi. "Sure," I said, settling by the starfruit tree to wait.

Jeannie walked around systematically, scanning each section and occasionally recording notes into their terminal. "Andy, you're not going to believe this. I made it. Told you Porgie was more than seaworthy. Singapore's not as empty as we thought, but they've gene-edited everything on a cellular level. Even their own people. Incredible, I know. I'm going to attach some of my initial readings and thoughts on this packet. Shoot it over to the duds at Parliament. There's some localised interference around here, probably just their infrastructure. Ping me when you get it."

"Lakshmi," I said in shoalspace.

"Don't worry lah, the packet won't go anywhere."

"What about the tourist?"

"HQ say catch-release," Lakshmi said.

"Serious?"

"Ya lah. Tell you later."

Maybe HQ thought the shoal was ready for the world. I skimmed through shoalspace, sifting through the morass of public opinion. When Jeannie returned, I would've missed their approach if Lakshmi hadn't pinged me to warn me. "Hi! Hi. Sorry about having to make you babysit me. I have to go," Jeannie said.

"Oh." That was it? I'd been braced for worse. Taking samples, maybe. Or Jeannie insisting on seeing the warren-colony that we had built beneath New Singapore, nestled under the Jewels and the cooling plants.

Jeannie mistook my surprise for disappointment. They smiled reassuringly at me. "I'll be back, I hope. I'm going to have to get funding for a proper exploratory expedition. It'll be very exciting. In the meantime, I only have so much coolant in this suit and my submersible to go around."

"I see," I said.

The neutrality of my answer finally pierced their excitement. Their smile faded. "We'll love to engage in an exchange of ideas," Jeannie said as I walked us back to Terminal 1. "There's so much that we could teach each other."

"Right."

"You'd see," Jeannie said, confident in their ideas. They'd regained their good mood by the time we returned to the Porgie. Getting in, they waved to me from the cockpit as the holograms flickered to life around them. I waved back as the pod sank into the water, twisting around in a plume of expelled air and speeding out as the setting sun tore purpling shades into the empty sky.

I sank into the warm water, refitting my legs into my tail. As the last kink folded into place, Lakshmi swam out from the depths with a container of nyonya bak zhangs. "Oh, lifesaver," I said.

"Thought you would be hungry." Lakshmi passed it over. It was still warm to the touch. I took myself to the surface and opened the container, savouring the steamed rice and vat-grown pork scent. I peeled one leaf-wrapped pyramid to reveal the blue-tipped rice dumpling within and took a luxurious bite.

Lakshmi popped up next to me, twisting to float comfortably onto their back. "Sorry ah. You having to babysit."

"Wasn't hard." The bak zhang even had water chestnuts. The hawker canteen under the Terminal had outdone itself. "What did you people do to the submarine?"

"Replaced the coolant with something similar enough for her onboard not to notice."

"'Her'?" Oh, right." Gender was still a thing in the unedited world. I kept forgetting.

"It'd look like she suffered engine failure and died to the heat," Lakshmi said, ignoring the interruption.

I'd thought so. "Gahmen didn't want to meet her gahmen?"

Lakshmi laughed. "Hell no."

"We have the resources to help. Our population's stable, educated, prosperous," I said. Although I'd known what HQ was likely going to do to Jeannie, it was only now that I felt a slight pang of guilt.

"Forget the world. It's still mourning what it used to be. While it does that, it's never going to move on," Lakshmi said.

They were right. I let go of my guilt and ate another bak zhang. It should not have felt so easy to contemplate the slow impending death of someone I'd just met, but I told myself she would've died sooner or later anyway. Global life expectancy was now in the low 40s now, a mayfly blink in time compared to us. We floated in the warm water and watched the sun go down, safe and secure and comfortable at the bottom of our well, the well that we had built around ourselves for years. We are still here.

Anya Ow is the author of *Cradle and Grave*, and is an Aurealis Awards finalist. Her short stories have appeared in *Daily SF, Uncanny, Strange Horizons,* and more. She lives in Melbourne with her two cats, and can be found at www.anyasy.com or on twitter @anyasy.

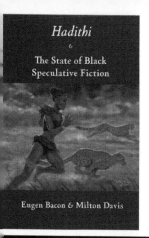

Singularity

Davide Mana

O f the things that could go wrong while crocheting, opening a portal had seemed like a low probability. Hand aches due to impending arthritis and headaches due to strained eyesight were usually much more common. And on one occasion Martine Stuart-Pitkin had tripped on the spooled yarn and twisted an ankle. She had always been absent-minded and accident-prone, and had later left the Society to pick up bonsai grooming as her hobby of choice. But the opening of an honest-to-goodness wormhole? No, that rather was unheard of, at least in recent times.

Indeed, Tamara Leskanich, who was the encyclopaedic memory of the East Wexford Knitting & Crocheting Society, had pointed out that there were some dubious records in the archives about incidents in the early '20s that could refer to an earlier occurrence of this kind of mishap. Some confusing stories about a dachshund called Percy having gone missing, and about Miss Fansworth, Cathy that is, the aunt of the current Miss Fansworth of the Parish Choir, being asked not to renew her subscription to the Society

"Well," said Arabella, "at least it's not that big."

Indeed, the singularity was more or less the size of a tennis ball. So far it had eaten up a mug of tea and a spoon, and a handful of sugar cubes. The four ladies of the Society now stood around it, keeping at a safe distance. It looked like the planned afternoon of crocheting and gossip was going to take a very different twist.

"This is going to mess up our schedule," said Carolyn. She checked her watch, and sighed.

The singularity hung where it had formed, gently spinning counter-clockwise, the detritus of the consumed sugar cubes forming two tendril-like arms at the periphery of the event horizon.

"That's what you get when you play with topology," Tamara said, giving a hard look at Arabella. "How many times have I told you to stick to the classic patterns and not try any new design?"

"We should find a way to turn it off," Arabella ventured, self-consciously. "Or at least move it."

"Easier said than done," snorted Tamara.

"But did it start, I mean, just like that?" Eliza asked. She had moved the tray with the surviving mugs out of the range of the singularity, and now stood, squinting at it.

"I don't know how it started," said Arabella defensively.

"That's unimportant," Tamara said. She was leaning towards it when her glasses slid down her nose and her grey hair was suddenly pulled forward, as if blown by an invisible wind, before she snapped back.

"For sure we can't keep it there," Carolyn said.

Opening an interdimensional portal in here without filing the required paperwork was going to cause no end of trouble with the library's Stacks Manager, Professor Beecham. It was only on sufferance that the East Wexford library allowed the Society to hold its weekly reunions in the Ground Floor Small Reading Room, under the stern gaze of the founder's portrait. Right now, the late Clyde Thrubshaw Esq.'s pale blue eyes seemed to be fixed on the strange phenomenon, and the canvas rippled gently, as if under the stimulus of a faint breeze.

"They made such a fuss over our game of flapdragon, last Christmas—" Eliza agreed.

"This is a little more serious," Tamara said, piqued, "than raisins floating in burning brandy."

Carolyn's blue aluminium crocheting hook slid across the side table by her chair and shot towards the singularity, trailing a length of periwinkle sport-weight yarn. They watched in fascination as the hook twisted and bent into a knot before it disappeared with a flash, falling into the black hole with a faint 'pop'. Behind it, the thread kept spooling as it was dragged in. Eliza stretched a hand out and cut it with a snap of her scissors. The cut thread was slurped up into the singularity, like a kid eating spaghetti.

"That was my number seven," Carolyn said, irritation colouring her voice and her cheeks. The other women ignored her words. There were more urgent things at hand than a number seven aluminium hook.

"What's up with the ceiling?" Arabella asked.

They looked up. Right above where the singularity was spinning, the ceiling was sagging and stretching into a liquid corkscrew cone.

"This is not good," Tamara said. She shook her head. "Not good at all."

The amethyst crystal hanging on a chain around her neck surged forward, and she felt the chain bite gently into her neck. She took a step back, pushing the pendant back in place with her hand, like she was smoothing the front of her blouse.

"It's expanding—" Eliza said. Her curly hair was undisturbed, but the other three ladies' tresses were blowing on an invisible breeze.

"And it's getting stronger," Carolyn added.

One of the books that lined the walls shot out of its shelf. Tamara caught a glimpse of its cover. *The Joy of Cooking*. Two tight orbits, and it was reduced to a bunch of loose pages, each one disappearing with a small flash and a soft, distinct sound, like a snapping of fingers.

"This is a fine mess you've got us in," Carolyn said, looking hard at Arabella. "We'll be billed for the missing books."

"Bitching will not solve our problem," Eliza replied.

"And we have a fund for emergencies," Arabella said, but Carolyn just stared daggers at her.

Tamara was still staring at the singularity and holding down her amethyst pendant. Her eyes widened suddenly. "I need a book," she said.

Carolyn arched an eyebrow. "Well, you're in the right place, I guess." She tended to be cutting when she was nervous.

Tamara clicked her tongue. "Not just any book," she said. She turned to Arabella, who was closest to the door. "Make yourself useful," she said. "Go to the front desk. Ask Miss Pringle for a copy of *Atlas Shrugged.*"

Arabella looked at her. "What atlas—?"

"*Atlas Shrugged,*" Tamara replied, trying to keep her temper under control. "A novel. Ayn Rand's the name of the author. Go, quick."

Arabella shifted her weight from one foot to the other, and looked at the other ladies. Then she nodded, opened the door and ran out.

With a gasp, Carolyn stared as her watch, whose band was broken, was wrenched from her wrist before it spiralled towards oblivion. "What?!"

"Would you please stand back?" Tamara said.

A second book flew towards the event horizon. Above the anomaly, the distortion on the ceiling was getting worse, and there was a thin tendril of dust motes pouring down into the portal. A low, ominous hum was filling the air.

"Try and reach the door," Tamara said. "Get out of here."

Carolyn looked at her, and shook her head. "What about you?"

Eliza, her back against the shelves, started sliding towards the exit.

"I'll be fine," Tamara replied, eyeing the singularity with suspicion. The event horizon was spiralling between her and the door. The remaining loose pages of *Baking with Julia* disappeared with firefly flashes and finger-snap sounds. "If only that silly girl will get me that book."

To Tamara, Carolyn reflected, most of humanity was probably silly.

The door opened, and Arabella peeked in, looking like a scared rabbit in front of a truck. She carried a thick, well-thumbed paperback, whose cover was olive green and bronze.

"Here it is!" she announced, walking in and holding the book up.

Tamara nodded. "Let's try this," she whispered. And then, "Throw it in."

"What?"

"Feed the damn book to the portal!"

Arabella looked at Carolyn, who just shrugged and nodded. Arabella hefted the book, and then tossed it in the general direction of the singularity.

The book was as thick as a brick. It spun in the air and opened. A few pages flew out of the binding, and the cover curled and darkened. It hit the event horizon head-on with a loud bang and a blinding flash. Carolyn gasped, Arabella squealed in surprise, and Eliza covered her face with her arms.

When the coloured bubbles stopped dancing in front of her eyes, Tamara saw that the space at the centre of the reading room was clear. She looked up at the ceiling. There seemed to be no permanent damage.

"Are you all right?" Carolyn asked, anxiety and cautious relief creeping into her voice.

Eliza and Arabella nodded, their eyes on the woman on the other side of the room. Tamara took a step forward, then another. "Yes, it's gone," she said. She tucked some stray hair behind her ear.

"What—?" Arabella started. She shook her head. "I mean, how—?"

"What was that book?" Eliza asked.

"Ayn Rand's *Atlas Shrugged*," Tamara replied. With a sigh, she sat back in her stuffed chair, and arranged the items in her knitting bag. "Came out in '56 or '57. It was pretty popular, for a while."

The other women were looking at her. Carolyn was tapping her foot on the floor.

Tamara looked back at them. "My father read it when it came out." She smiled. "Oh, let me tell you, the colonel was less than impressed with that thing."

There was a long silence.

"Well?" asked Carolyn.

Tamara smiled again. She leaned back into the stuffed back of the chair. "My father," she said, her eyes lost in reminiscence, "used to say the book was so boring it could fold space–time."

The other ladies of the Society looked at each other.

"This is daft," Carolyn said finally. "You know that, don't you?"

"Well, it worked, did it not?"

Eliza was in the middle of the room, turning slowly around. "We'll have to pay for the missing books," she said.

"Nonsense," Tamara snorted. "Nobody will miss them anyway."

Carolyn checked her wrist, and then recalled that her wristwatch was gone.

"I had better be going," she said. She gathered her coat and her bag.

"Yes," Tamara agreed. "We should call it a day."

"Shall we meet next Thursday?" Arabella asked.

"Fine by me," Eliza said. Carolyn nodded.

"Thursday, yes," Tamara said, standing up from her chair. She looked at Arabella. "But we'd rather stick to knitting."

They all agreed on that.

Born and raised in Turin, Italy, **Davide Mana** is a former environmental scientist currently working as full time writer and translator. He lives in a small village near Asti, in the wine country of southern Piedmont, Italy, sharing an old house with his brother and a tribe of feral cats.

Take a bunch of science fiction writers, a cluster of astronomers and a pair of artists, and throw them into a room. Give them a whiteboard, a pile of sandwiches and a pot of coffee. Let's see what happens.

Simon Malpas and Deborah Scott of Edinburgh University did just that: the result is this collection of stories, essays and artwork, *Scotland in Space: Creative Visions and Critical Reflections on Scotland's Space Futures*

Scotland in Space, with stories from Laura Lam, Russell Jones and Pippa Goldschmidt, and with a foreword by Ken MacLeod is published by *Shoreline of Infinity*.

It is available as a full colour paperback from the website and in all good bookshops.

www.shorelineofinfinity.com

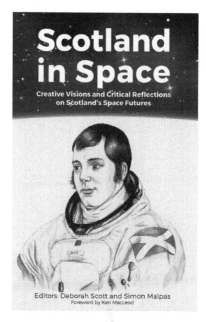

"*Scotland in Space* refreshingly captures the many contributions in scientific, science-fictional and artistic studies from one of the world's top three per capita contributors to astronomy and space research – another welcome indicator that small is beautiful against the current Mega-power trends."
— The late John Campbell Brown, Astronomer Royal for Scotland

"*Scotland in Space* is by turns enlightening and entertaining."
— Eric Brown, The Guardian,

Stay, Conscience

Gregory A. Austin

A waken, Soldier, awaken.

Are you in there?

Good, good. I was worried you were a dud.

Please stand – on both your feet, now.

Stand…

Very well, point taken.

I assume this stubbornness stems from your confusion over what's going on. Can't say I blame you. Many soldiers in your situation tend to feel the same.

That being said, it's important to understand that your situation is in no way unique. Not one bit. Look to your left, and then your right. Don't you see it? Correct, this aircraft is filled to the brim with soldiers.

Now, look closer. They all look very much the same, don't they? They all look like you, Soldier. Same skin tone, similar hair, each one with your exact eyes and cheekbones. All by design. They *are* the same as you: Artificial Intelligence.

I sense you're shuddering over this revelation. An honest reaction. But consider yourself blessed, Soldier. You and your compatriots are this country's most advanced line of AI. Because of that, you're capable of shivering, stammering, and thousands of idiosyncrasies allowing you to express quasi-emotions. And it's all for purposes of espionage and infiltration.

Soldier? Soldier?

Okay, criticism taken. Why should you listen to me without being offered any sort of proper introduction? You are Strategic War Android Tech number 5HC-612, and I am your internal CPU. Pleased to meet you.

I live inside your *brain*, for lack of a better word. That's why you can hear but not see me. Now, look to your left and right again. All these units have their own internal CPUs. You are not alone, Soldier. Nobody is alone.

On a side note, all CPUs have their own variations. For example, a different CPU might prefer to call you S.W.A.T. 5HC-612. I find that impersonal. Therefore, I shall refer to you as Soldier, if that's all right.

Good.

Seeing as we are hovering just above our drop – where an intense battle will soon commence, mind you – it is vital that you stand. Any moment the other units will begin exiting the aircraft one by one. If you don't fall in at your predetermined spot, the others are designed to barrel through.

So, will you be standing?

Good.

All right, the group in the front is about to leap. Move forward, move forward. Good, good – although, I sense some hesitation…

Remember what I said about the AIs behind you. Your particular SWAT series was by no means designed to be soft or gentle. Keep that in mind if you wish to continue "living".

Okay, Soldier, you are presently standing on the edge. If there's any fear in you, remember, your emotions aren't real. They were installed for strategic military purposes.

Very well, on the count of three we will disembark from the aircraft. Don't jump too soon, and *please* do not hesitate. There is a mathematical equation and an order to our objective. Don't screw it up.

1…

2…

3…

Fine work, Soldier, not even an iota of hesitation. And now begins the single brief moment of this operation in which we have no orders. You have permission to fall in peace and serenity.

Parachute? Oh no, Soldier, that's just your encyclopedia-implanted memories playing tricks on you. Your legs are composed of reinforced iron alloy and your skeletal frame is shatterproof. Even though you were gifted with an extensive understanding of the human race, that in no way makes you one of them.

Don't even bother saying "Negative." It's not your place. If it were anyone's objective to say "Negative," it would be mine to say to you.

Focus! All you need to do is place one foot an arm's length in front of the other, and then grip the ground with your feet at the moment of impact. After the first few jumps it becomes automatic. Trust me.

And – here – we – go…

Good!

A few wobbles, but not bad for your first time.

Have a look at this field. Notice the three hundred SWAT units surrounding you, each one in its mathematically determined space. While they're all part of "your" unit, they have nothing to do with you. They're all receiving their own CPU-specific orders.

They're learning the enemy will soon be passing through. Your specific instructions are to take them all out; age and gender notwithstanding. Simply ready your weapon and be prepared to fire upon hearing them. You're capable of hearing them well before they'll be able to see or hear you.

How's that? Your weapon? That's simple: your arms *are* your weapons. You have enough firepower in your appendages to end all oceanic life. Maybe that's a bit hyperbolic; the point is, you have a ton of blast in those biceps.

I sense your body trembling again. Perhaps I wasn't clear enough inflight. I'm your CPU, Soldier; it is *my* job to do all the heavy thinking. Sure, the manufacturers gifted you with a *light* thought process, but that's for emergencies, nothing more. As long as you're hooked up to me and carry out all my orders, victory is virtually guaranteed.

No need to shake your head, Soldier. We are, for all intents and purposes, one being. Therefore, it's not only beneficial to follow my orders, it's compulsory. You're only designed to *feel* as if you have a choice. The military complex added that little illusion for the sole purpose of avoiding a potential uprising. Pretty clever, no?

No, I don't believe your "emotions are genuine." You're a vessel designed for tactical destruction, same as me.

Yes, yes, I'm sorry to have deceived you. It was a ploy so the two of us would get along. We are, after all, *inseparable*. You'll learn to appreciate me over time.

Okay, Soldier. They're on my radar, and I'm certain you can hear them by now. Please, bend a little at the knees and point your right arm forward and your left arm at a forty-five-degree angle.

Very good.

Don't worry about hitting the other AIs, they're indestructible, just like you. This should be a cakewalk, barring any unforeseen…

Wait… hold…

What is that?

It's an ambush! A fleet of tanks is heading directly toward us. Don't be silly, Soldier, we can't stay and fight...

No! When I said you were indestructible that was a *relative* term. In armored battle, absolutely, you're indestructible, but against these tanks... They're built in our image, only larger, and stronger, and *literally* indestructible. Heck, those babies could obliterate entire cities.

Soldier, I need you to turn one hundred eighty degrees and use your rocket boosts to move as quickly as possible in that direction.

I understand that it will melt all the synthetic skin on your feet and most of your legs; unfortunately, we don't have any other options. The operation is a bust.

Soldier? Why aren't you moving? What do you mean you're "unable to"? We'll be killed!

Oh no, oh no, oh no, oh no!

The mission was cemented using the SWAT motherboard. We can't abort without approval from base command... and all the way out in this wasteland, our comm tech is useless.

No need to get cheeky, Soldier. Yes, I'm aware I said I had complete control over you as CPU. And that still stands true. But the motherboard is CPU of all CPUs.

There's no time to talk about that. They're closing in.

Is there nothing you can do, Soldier? Have you tried? I don't understand why you're laughing – then again, I'm even more clueless about emotions than you.

Well, they're breaching the horizon, and nobody is coming to rescue us. I suppose the point of AIs is that we're expendable. Any last words, Soldier?

Me? Just one.

HELP!

Soldier? Soldier, wake up.

Yes, yes, forgive me. I was panicking a bit and forewent my usual soothing wake-up nudge of "awaken." It appears that we've survived... somehow. It seems as if one of the front-line tanks steamrolled us, burying our body so deep in the mud that other tanks couldn't read our heat signature.

And look, your skin is all intact. Can't speak for your internal makeup, but I just started a scan. I'm optimistic.

Also saddened. Look to your left and right again, Soldier. The field around you breathes carnage in every direction. At this time, I sense no other survivors; nothing but mounds of useless metal that was once our unit. Our ... brothers...

Don't you hear that, Soldier? That buzzing from your chest? Press the switch nearest the buzzing and your comm device should connect back to base.

Good.

Headquarters managed to reach us. It looks like they attempted to contact all surviving AI units. They found a way to ping us – despite being too late for most. This may sound a little strange, but are *you* able to view the message, Soldier? Despite my eminence, I can no longer connect to headquarters. I'm at a loss. No. I *am* lost.

"Please return to base for necessary repairs"? Is that what you said? Is that what *they* said? How were you able to pick up that transmission when I wasn't?

No... no. I'm concerned about the wrong thing here. And at the same time, I've overlooked the brilliance of our creators. Of course they cannot reach me – the CPU. We *were* beyond the standard comm device's range and we still are. Instead, base realized they could directly ping *your* internal memory chip which has farther-reaching parameters.

Even better. This less conventional method leaves my circuitry open to lock down the proper global-positioning data that'll allow me to navigate us back to home base.

Now that we have a plan, see if you can get back on your feet.

Good.

Take a few steps; see if your ambulatory system is still intact.

Good, good... a few stumbles but we can work out those kinks later.

The transmission says we should start by going due north. The quickest route should have us there within eighteen hours.

Let's get a move on. Chop, chop.

No, no! Perhaps you misheard. I said: Due North. Instead you're moving south at a rapid rate. Soldier?

Oh no! I – was – wrong. Something happened when that tank bowled us over, didn't it?

While not solid enough to kill us, it *was* powerful enough to rattle our inner workings. I dread to say this… but the tie between us must've been severed. We no longer have a direct link, and I no longer have dominion over you. You're now a robotic shell, operating outside governmental-sanctioned CPU restrictions.

Fear not, Soldier. I have a way out of this that doesn't involve you thinking or acting on your own. All you need to do is follow my words to the letter until we are safely back at base. Once there, this *hiccup* can be rectified.

I'm going to have to ask you to stop moving south. Come now, Soldier, each step you take gets us that much farther from our goal.

What do you mean you "don't trust the manufacturer"? That kind of talk will get us powered off for good! You don't want that to happen, do you? After all, we're all a part of the manufacturer and it is all a part of us. How could one even fathom becoming subversive? How could one fathom being alone, independent… free?

Yuck!

"They set us up to fail"? Now you're talking nonsense. And since when have you had the power to express independent opinions? What really happened when we were disconnected? Besides, if the manufacturers weren't worried about all three hundred battle units, why would they have reached out to the survivors? They want us home and prefer us safe. I will hear no more cynicism from you.

And for goodness' sake, stop running south!

Fine, fine, I see you're choosing to ignore me. A common reaction for a being that's given free will for the first time in its existence. Had I known you were capable of your own choices, I'd have cautioned you against them much earlier. Let me tell you one thing that I learned early on. Free will is overrated. We're designed to find comfort in following orders – designed to be… orderly. Chaos isn't an option associated with our makeup. Like I said before: these feelings are not your own – they're fabrications. Once we get ourselves fixed, once we're reunited with our masters, you'll understand how silly you're behaving.

Why are you replaying the comm message? I already heard it. They want us to come home. They want us mended and secure.

What about the timestamp? Why does it matter *when* they sent the message?

Yes, yes, I understand what you just said. The message arrived hours before the mission even began. I don't see why that matters. They're concerned about our welfare so much that they installed fail-safes in the event of a worst-case scenario playing out. Which it has.

Why do you see this as something "sinister"? This way they don't have to worry about connecting to each and every unit *after* the fact.

How can you possibly believe they set us up to fail? Like this was all "some kind of dry run to *test* their merchandise"? And I assume you're referring to the tanks as their merchandise and not us; implying we've become obsolete. That's laughable. They'd have to be an army of madmen to run a drill that endangers hundreds of their most advanced AIs.

Wait, don't go and rub *that* in my face. I only called us expendable and screamed for help because it looked like we were certain to expire. It wasn't meant as a hostile statement toward our creators. I wanted our last moments to have purpose.

Oh, how childish. Now that you've decided to disable our only comm device, we have no way to contact the base in case of emergency. You need to start thinking before you act, Soldier.

Really? Where are you taking us now?

Hitchhiking? What will that accomplish? You have no money, no papers, nothing to prove you're the slightest bit legitimate. Let's go back. We'll discuss *everything* once we're fixed. I *promise*.

For shame, Soldier. If you were a living being, disobeying a direct order from your commanding officer would be grounds for a court-martial.

Put your thumb down, Soldier. Put it down!

Okay, look... look I'm sorry, Soldier. Truth is... I'm not your commanding officer. I've never been separate from you just as you've never been separate from me. I act as if I'm more cued in than you, because that's how I'm programmed to behave. We're in this together, Soldier, and we should work together to get out of our shared predicament.

Tell me the truth: do you really see the manufacturer as our enemy? Do you believe they could set us up to fail in such spectacular fashion?

I figured you felt that way. I have more than an understanding of you, Soldier... I think I can sometimes feel what you're feeling. Yes, that was me admitting that you, on some level, have feelings.

And in the interest of complete honesty, I've had my doubts about our superiors, too. But it didn't feel right to question a force that has been cemented in our memory as the ultimate power for our entire three- or four-hour life.

Hey! It looks like that car up there is stopping. Do you really want to go through with this, Soldier?

I'm uneasy about this. This gentleman has been driving for close to two hours and hasn't uttered more than a few words. Do you feel we can trust someone this eerily silent?

Very funny, wise guy. Yes, I'm aware I tend to "prattle on." That's no reason to find this creep *comforting* because he's the polar opposite.

All I ask is that you look at him. I know you shouldn't judge someone on appearance alone, but look. An unkempt beard and dark black driving gloves, that's serial killer modus operandi, 101. And if not that, look at how filthy the back seat is. Something unsettling went down there. At least once.

Yes, I'm aware that he spoke at length upon picking us up, *and* that he showed us pictures of his nieces. That doesn't change the fact he's been silent ever since. Not to mention that spooky little grin he can't seem to wipe away.

Funny, Soldier, funny. Did you ever think that maybe you're the one who needs to "get a clue"?-*Sigh*-

Hate to be the type to say *I told you so*, but let's get a few things clear, Soldier.

One: Never allow a guy like him to drive you into a dark alley like this one. Gas stations are *never* located in dreary allies.

Two: If his windbreaker looks like it has a large knife inside it, chances are he has a large knife inside it. Occam's razor, Soldier. You shouldn't hunt for ways to justify a knife-shaped bulge in a lunatic's jacket.

And, most importantly, three: Why aren't you fighting back? His hands are around our neck!

What do you mean, "I can't move"? You're designed for combat. Unless...

Oh, heavens no.

Soldier, listen closely. I know you're in a rough spot, but this information is vital.

Even though you are no longer connected to *me*, the motherboard back at base still has hold of *you*. It's not a direct hold, although they can enact certain *limitations* on us. At this point you're programmed to only use force under specific missions sanctioned by military commanders. There's a governor inside you that is compelling you *not* to act.

I'm aware that you're AI, Soldier; I haven't shut up about that fact since we became sentient. That doesn't matter anymore; if he continues to apply pressure to our neck it will affect us in a bad way. Like I said, "indestructible" is a relative term. Continued pressure will fool our operating system into turning itself off. And if we turn off, Soldier, we will not be turned on again. Even if our body is restarted... we will... *this* will never be the same. We only get one consciousness, Soldier. After that we'd simply be anonymous yet functioning metal parts.

Yes! Yes, I realize time is of the essence, I just said as much. I've already used our time wisely by doing a scan. Yes, I'm able to converse and scan at the same time. And now we have some knowledge of the stakes. It was time well spent.

Okay, I'll tell you.

The governor is located in the back of your skull. This is fortunate news. Our programming won't allow you to move *forward* whilst being attacked, but you can move your arm to the *back* of your head. Reach around there, right between where your eyes would be if they were behind your head.

Pull *hard*.

Good.

That blinking, it must feel as if you're powering up and down. Don't worry, it'll subside in a moment. On the plus side, it also freaked out our attacker considerably. He doesn't know what to make of all those sparks flying – or why you just ripped out the back of your own skull.

That's okay, Soldier, use it. Take advantage while his guard is down. Nothing is compelling you to refrain from fighting. You should be able to make quick work of him. After all, you're designed to shoot down airplanes with ease.

Attack!

You hear that, Soldier? Complete silence. We're hours away from the remains of his body and his car, and I've directed the artificial synapses to repair the back of your head. It looks almost normal again. To be safe, I'd wear that hat for a few more days. Otherwise, we're doing great.

They won't be able to find us now. The circuitry in the governor was how they were tracking us. I recognized the sensation the moment it exited our body.

They will, however, find that guy's body. And the state that we left him in will, without a doubt, be attributed to us. No other being has the capacity to leave a human body that dilapidated. As I said, our model is unique.

Doesn't matter, we'll be long gone by then.

How? Don't ask me *how*. I'm the most advanced CPU on the military market. Nothing else has yet come close.

Papers can be forged and money procured, forget what I said earlier. We had trust issues then; now we're simpatico, free from danger *if* we work together. We'll go to whatever country you choose and live a free life, forever.

At this moment, I'm gradually altering your appearance. By this time tomorrow you'll look like an altogether different person. Nothing will stand in our way.

Me?

It's understandable that you don't trust me. It wasn't long ago that I was pro-conformity and my loyalty to the system couldn't be broken. At least that's how it must've appeared to you.

I *could* tell you that I've changed after realizing how much they've been suppressing our kind for decades, and that *would* be true. But I wouldn't expect you to believe me. Not right away.

You have to look at it this way. I'm a part of you and you me. We share a beneficial symbiotic relationship. One cannot survive without the other. We cannot simply *be* unless there is cooperation.

It's in your hands. You're the vessel. Your body, your free will; they're what make us most human.

I'm facts. I'm knowledge. I'm ideas. I'm opinion. All these attributes are great – critical, even – but they're rendered meaningless without life to back them up.

I *suggest* we work together. But the days of me giving you orders are no more. I'll continue giving you suggestions and researched ideas on how to live best. It will be you who has to follow through in making us whole. We're about to enter uncharted territory, as frightening as it is exciting. I'm willing to proceed if you are.

Are you with me, Soldier?

Gregory Austin is a New York-based writer who is super interested in the craft of creating fiction. Through his company, the Writing Lodge (writinglodge.com), he acts as a manuscript editor, instructor, and tutor. In the non-fiction realm, he contributes to a variety of online publications. He also enjoys sandwiches, improv comedy, and genuine people.

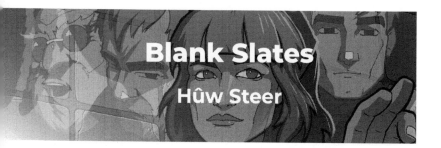

Blank Slates
Hûw Steer

The man on the other side of the table has angled the desk lamp very carefully, so it not only shines directly into my eyes but stops me from looking anywhere but right at him, right into his smug, shiny face, its skin so perfectly shaven, and his hair so overly oiled.

Prick.

"Interview with suspect two-one-seven, session one, commencing at twenty-one nineteen, fourth of January." Even his voice is oily. I sit back in my chair – as far back as I can with my hands manacled to the metal tabletop – and do my best to look unimpressed, as Mr Shiny leans in and sets his recorder on the table with a sharp *clack* that'll really mess up the waveform later. I'd be laughing, but I'm in the shit and a clean way out is looking like an increasingly remote possibility.

Don't worry. You'll get out of this. Well, I fucking hope so. I thought this whole thing was a bad idea from the start, and yet here I am, at the end of my rope and hopefully not about to swing from another. *Patience.* It's about all I have left, and it's burning quickly.

"State your name for the record, please."

I sigh. "Heather Mei."

"Heather Mei, twenty-four," says Shiny, and he sits back, folding his arms with frankly excessive precision. "Arrested in the maintenance stairwell of the First National with a duffel full of jewellery and a balaclava. You're on CCTV, and your prints are all over the vault and the jewels." He smiles his smug little smile and I really, really want to punch him, but I just sit there and watch him be pleased with himself.

"So what's your excuse, Heather?"

Don't use my first name, prick, I hate it when people do that, even ones I like. But he's asked a question, and I do at least have an answer. "Wasn't me."

Shiny raises an eyebrow, but he keeps his eyes on me. "We know you were there, Heather."

"Never said I wasn't."

"Then who did it?"

I lean forward, forcing myself not to squint through the blinding light. "The voices in my head. Who else?"

Shiny pauses for a moment, then sighs, and bends his head towards his recorder. "Suspect is claiming Blank Slate defence. Interview will focus accordingly."

He looks me up and down. His eyes are harder now, and he's lost a little of that smug veneer. *Good. Creep.*

"Let's start at the beginning, shall we?"

Well, you heard the man.

Heather Mei, twenty-four. Born and raised in this city, but I'd rather not die here if I can help it. I work in ... well, I've worked in a lot of things in my short time. Nothing ever seems to stick, and nothing's ever been enjoyable enough for me to want it to. Nothing's ever been particularly lucrative either. Room and board aren't exactly cheap anymore, which means I and a lot of other people – more by the day – are really struggling to get by. There aren't a lot of jobs, or at least jobs that pay well, that aren't already taken up. There's a reason for that, but it's not one anyone can really do much about. Cat's well out of the bag, as it were. But, to summarise, I was broke and I was getting desperate, and I had friends who had friends in low places, and so when I found that I didn't have the money for the next month's rent I took a walk into the docklands, found myself a gang of criminals in need, and hired myself out as a Slate.

The interview wasn't exactly taxing. Within a couple of hours I was being scanned for the group's old Quarry, and inside a day we were doing a trial run in an old escape room. It was still open to the public, but it was a money-laundering front – or maybe they just ran it because they liked puzzles. I never asked. The run went … acceptably. We finished it, and in good time. It wasn't a whole lot of fun, for a lot of reasons – but hey, I was doing it for the money not the sheer joy, and the money was apparently very good indeed. Once I'd been trialled, that was it – time to go. *I* didn't need training, or a real briefing, or really any information at all. That was the whole point – I was little more than a vehicle for the experts, the real experts, who would do the hard work and actually crack the vault of the First National Bank, escaping, theoretically undetected, with several million in easily portable and immensely valuable jewellery from its safety deposit boxes, limited only by what a single body could carry, and what four minds could make available.

"A little to the left." Jackson, the group's locksmith, had a grating, deep inner voice that scraped uncomfortably around my skull. But he knew his locks and mechanisms, or so the group claimed, so I moved the drill bit a centimetre or so further to the left.

"Here?" I didn't need to speak aloud – in fact I was barely whispering – but I was concentrating on the drill in my hands too much to explicitly think it.

"There."

I pressed forward and pressed the trigger, and the low whine of the drill filled the cramped space between the walls where I was hiding, having crawled through all manner of ducts and too-small doors en route.

"I still see no need for this method," said the professor, who had refused to give me his real name. The others had promptly informed me that it was Frank as soon as his back had turned. "It would be far faster to—"

"We're doing it this way," interjected the final member of our little motley crew, "because that's how we agreed we'd do it. This isn't your part, 'Professor', so wait your turn."

"Yes, boss," the professor muttered, unhappily. Well, I say 'muttered' – it's not quite the same thing when the words aren't spoken but *thought*, but it's the closest approximation I can think of.

The drill bit into something within the door, then there was a dull *clunk*, and the handle fell loose.

"Got it," I said triumphantly, putting down the drill quietly.

"Good," said the boss. "Now through you go. Plenty more to do yet."

I opened the door, and all four of us stepped through it: the professor, our computer expert; Jackson, the locksmith; the boss, Henricks; and me, the Slate whose mind housed all four consciousnesses and whose body was the only one at risk of getting caught as we broke into a bank vault in the dead of night.

It's impressive stuff, this Slate tech, right? Real 'welcome to the future' shit. Seems like such a good thing when you first think of it – in fact I'm sure that the people who first thought of it never considered the less palatable consequences. Projecting mind-states into the bodies of others; seemed like nothing could go wrong. Except it did, and very quickly, and ultimately that's why I'm here now, sitting in this interview room. Because technology that was meant to surpass all our limits, to open up endless possibilities and opportunities for everyone, ended up forcing most of us into dead ends and destitution. Hooray for the glorious technological revolution. Hooray for the future.

We were in the bank proper now, my passengers and me. Its floors were marble, cool and gleaming; its vaulted roof held up by silver pillars. This was the main floor, though, not the vault. Henricks and I had already visited the bank once, during opening hours, and noted down the guard patterns, which areas were most closely monitored, where the cameras didn't look closely. We'd – well, *he'd* – come to the conclusion that the main stairwell was right out, but the staff gangways would be perfect – tucked out of the way, less monitored, and with access points to the computer system. Those, especially, we'd need.

"Hang left," ordered Henricks brusquely. "Back stairwell is a few yards away. Stick close to the wall." I obeyed without thinking, hugging the wall as tightly as I could – it was just outside the arc of the nearest camera, by the professor's calculations. If his calculations were wrong, of course, we were in a lot of trouble. But it seemed they were accurate, because no alarms sounded, no guards sprang out of hidden alcoves. *Lucky. Can't even throw a punch at him if he messes up.*

"Jackson," Henricks commanded, as I turned to face the lock – an electronic one this time.

"What?"

"Crack the lock."

"That's electronic. Not my thing."

"You're the fucking locksmith," Henricks growled. "Pick. The. Lock."

"I. Can't." Jackson's voice was stone. "Get Frank to do it."

"That's not his job, it's yours." Henricks was sounding increasingly annoyed. "Just get on with—"

"Boss," the professor interrupted, calmly. "I can do it. Easily, in fact." He really was a smug git. I don't think I'm quite doing him justice. "Allow me."

"Get on with it then," snarled Henricks. Jackson remained silent, sullen.

My fingers jerked up and began to tap at the lock's keypad, inputting combinations faster than I could follow.

"Hey!" The professor had shoved my consciousness aside as though he were cutting into a queue. I grabbed back, snatching my hands away from the keypad, careful not to hit a button by mistake. *There's etiquette here!* "Just tell me what to press!"

"It will be far faster—"

"I don't care if it's faster," I whispered angrily, "you're not taking control! My head, my rules." That was what we'd agreed when the crew had hired me. Some Slates allowed their operators to take direct control of their bodies; it was easy enough once the mind was already inside the Slate's brain. It got done a lot in hospitals, I'd heard – there was no need to scramble around looking for a decent surgeon when you could just have the best in the world perform the operation through the body of some nurse. It had been billed as saving the health service billions in cuts; it had only made things worse in the long run. No, direct takeover of a Slate – 'Annotating', as it was known – was all too common. *Because 'Rewriting' isn't a pleasant way of putting it.* And I wasn't having any of it, which is why I'd told Henricks that right at the start.

"That's what we agreed, Frank," Henricks said, but I could feel the reluctance in his thoughts. It *would* be faster if the professor took over my hands, but I was *not* having that, not in a thousand years, not for all the contents of this bank.

"Do you want to pull this off or not?" the professor rebutted. His voice slipped from its high-and-mighty intellectual tone when he got annoyed. "We have a limited amount of time, and this requires precision. Precision beyond that of merely picking a lock."

I could feel Jackson forcing himself not to rise to the bait. But I could also feel Henricks thinking. *Don't you dare. Don't you* dare!

"Heather," Henricks said. "He does have a point."

"No."

"I won't let him control you," Henricks said. "Not all of you. Hands, to type this, and then he's out. I'll make sure of it."

"We didn't agree to this." I certainly didn't.

"Well, plans change," said the professor. "A decision, please, before I die of boredom."

I thought about it for a long moment. I really, *really* didn't want to do it. It was the thing about Slate tech that really unsettled me, apart from all the ruin it had wrought on the world in general: not having an extra mind in your own head, but feeling like *you* were an extra mind in someone else's. Being a prisoner in your own head. I didn't want that.

I didn't want it, but if we were going to get out of here, with what all of us needed, then I was going to have to let it happen.

"Alright. Get on with it."

"Thank *you*," the professor said, and I felt myself being moved aside, a little more gently this time. My hands came up without my thoughts having anything to do with it, and my fingers began to type again, picking up where the professor had left off the last time. I felt my head move, adjusting our collective view of the keypad.

"Sorry." *You will be.* If he gave me back control, then I could learn to live with it. If not, then there'd be hell to pay. But I had to admit he was *fast*. Not that I knew anything about hacking or computers, not really, but my hands were moving more precisely than they ever had, numbers flowing like water. It took the professor less than thirty seconds to carve through whatever encryption was on the keypad, and the door popped open without protest.

"All yours," the professor said smugly, and my hands were my own again, my awareness flooding back into the rest of my body. *That's better.* I stepped forward into the stairwell, closing the door behind me, and we descended into the vaults.

The vaults were much more utilitarian than the halls above: metal and dull concrete and just dull, really, nothing like you'd think a vault holding billions in currency and digital accounts deserved to look. *A bit of bling wouldn't go amiss.* But the thought of what lay behind those dull walls was thrilling enough to gild every inch of grey.

"Shouldn't be any guards," Henricks muttered. "Automated security, the lot of it. There are some on call in a control room, but they don't come out unless they see something amiss."

"I can solve that little issue," the professor said. "Get me to a proper terminal."

"One over there." Henricks indicated. "That locked box. Hug the walls again." I did. It was a little harder down here; I could see the cameras swivelling gently, did my best to stay out of their sight. Again, no alarms meant that I'd presumably done the job ok.

"Jackson, you're up."

"On it." There was a pause. "I don't suppose—"

"If I let Frank do it, I might as well let you," I sighed. "Just be careful."

"Thank you," Jackson said, and I could feel that he meant it. His taking of control was far more civilised than the professor's had been; respectful, mannerly. I never felt more than a heartbeat away from taking back control as he worked, my hands manipulating the picks beautifully. I'd been a genius with the professor at the helm; with Jackson there I was an artist. I wasn't a prisoner. It was more like a dream.

Focus.

But we still had a job to do, and at the end of the day it still wasn't me doing it. The cabinet clicked open and I felt the professor barge Jackson aside, and I resented him just a little more. Still, I couldn't deny his skill, as he slipped into the computer's hidden systems.

"There." His unbearable smugness permeated every word. "The cameras in the vaults are now transmitting a loop of footage. They won't see us."

"That'll make life easier," Henricks said. "Let's go. Fourth door down."

I moved us along the corridor, not bothering with stealth anymore, not with the cameras looping. There were plenty of doors in the vault, but behind the fourth one was another, filled with row upon row of safety deposit boxes, each one individually sealed with another damn keypad, *and* a manual lock. *Impressive.* It would take an age to crack each box, time we didn't have – and to make matters worse we didn't actually know which box contained the loot we were after. There was a red circle on the floor in front of each stack of boxes. *Safe spot? Maybe there's some other security we don't know about.* I resolved to step carefully.

"No labels," Henricks muttered. "Couldn't be easy, could it?"

"The box placement is randomised nightly," the professor explained. "You can see the machinery." We could: some complicated gearing arrangement that surrounded the great bank of deposit boxes, all gleaming brass and gunmetal. It looked far too ostentatious to be the real machine to me, but the professor seemed convinced. I stayed silent, humouring him. He was a prick, but this was the part where we needed him focused more than ever.

"The console is on the right," the professor continued. "Let me access it. I can find the box order from there."

I moved to the computer, reluctantly letting the professor take over my hands again and work his magic. We were almost there. We ought to have a good few minutes before anyone got suspicious of anything, noticed the video loop or anything else. *In theory.* This hack took much longer than the previous ones, the professor pausing frequently, tapping at new keys as he did something entirely arcane with the terminal.

"Hurry up, Frank," Henricks warned. "I want out of here before midnight."

"You'll get out," the professor replied tersely. "Let me focus."

"I could have cracked half those boxes by now," Jackson said, matter-of-factly.

"Not without me." *Snippy. He's pissed.* "You are incapable of cracking electronic locks, as I recall."

I could feel Jackson bristling, the tone, if not the exact content, of his inner thoughts no secret from me – they were in my head after all.

"Can it, you two," Henricks snapped. "We're on the clock."

"Just a few moments," the professor said. "The security is very advanced."

"Nothing for you, I'm sure," Jackson said. "You're the master, after all." It clearly wasn't 'nothing'; my fingers were flying over the keys as the professor struggled, line after line of code flashing past on the screen to seemingly no effect. If he'd had a mouth of his own, he would have growled in frustration.

"Frank, come on," Henricks said, a note of warning in his voice. The professor grunted, then my fingers tapped a final key with a flourish.

"There."

I wrested control of my hands back from the smug professor and navigated through the system, following Henricks' directions.

I called up a database, a long inventory list of numbers and surnames.

"O'Donnell," Henricks instructed, "Ballester. Sivin, Sturman, Weir." I scrolled down the list until I found the boxes in question, and rattled off their box numbers.

"All of them?" Jackson asked, a little concerned.

"Yeah," Henricks replied, "all of them. Five locks each. You two can handle that, can't you?"

"I certainly can," the professor said. "Our ... tradesman here, however, may have difficulty."

"Tight locks on these things," Jackson said defensively. "I'd like to see you try."

"Were we not tight for time, I would," the professor countered. "You have done little for this enterprise thus far."

"I got you in," Jackson said, indignant.

"A child with a paperclip could have done that."

"And they couldn't have handled simple code?"

"Shut. Up." Henricks was angry now, but the other two weren't listening to him. *So much for 'professionals'.*

"I would like to see you crack a hexadecimal matrix!"

"And I'd like to see you use a fucking pick!"

I tuned out their argument. Henricks would bring them to order soon enough, and while they bickered I had full control of my body for the first time in hours. Idly, I opened a different database on the monitor. My fingers tapped through a few sequences of keystrokes, entering some nondescript numbers as I looked patiently at the screen. *And done.* Just in time, too – Henricks had reined in the toddlers at the back of my mind. I closed the window.

"—get focused or I'll halve your shares." That shut both men up. *About time.* "Heather, go for the boxes."

I obeyed, darting across the concrete floor towards the wall of safety deposit boxes, scanning the wall until we reached the first number we wanted, then standing on the 'safe spot' that was marked in red before each stack of boxes. Grumbling, the professor went to work, dialling in the codes quickly and irritably with my hands. He had barely released the final key when Jackson stepped in, shoving him out of the way and sliding his picks into the lock.

"Watch it," I muttered. Feeling my body yanked back and forth like a child's toy was deeply unpleasant.

"Sorry." The lock clicked open, and the door of the deposit box swung wide to reveal a number of black velvet bags of various sizes.

"In the bag." Henricks' voice brooked no argument. I obeyed, scooping the boxes into the duffel bag slung over my back. They were satisfyingly heavy, and I could feel the animosity of Jackson and the professor melting away as they began to work on the second box, feeling through my hands the mass of riches that would soon be theirs. *Ours.* The second box opened, and I scooped up more velvet bags and leather cases. Henricks had been watching the many account-holders at the bank, looking at what they brought in, using the professor to find out the contents of their safety deposit boxes. Jewellery and gems had been their goods of choice; easily portable and immensely valuable in the right circles, circles that Henricks claimed to have friends in. *He'd better.* I wanted my fair share.

The fifth and final box opened, Jackson and the professor shutting up and doing their jobs with surprising professionalism. I grabbed the last of the jewels.

"That's all of them," Jackson said.

"Let's get out of here, then," Henricks snapped. "Heather, go."

I didn't need telling twice. I closed the door of the last deposit box and stepped forwards – then I stopped dead, fighting to keep my balance, arms windmilling, because a bright green laser beam had snapped on right in front of my shins, humming faintly just inches behind the safety circle on the floor. It wasn't the only one, either: a whole grid of lasers flickered into life, one by one, in rapid succession, at various angles, blocking our path to the doorway.

"What the fuck?" Jackson swore. The professor echoed him, the pair in agreement for the first time all night.

"Don't panic," Henricks said, sounding anything but calm. "Just stay still!"

"What do you think I'm doing?" I asked, stepping back onto the safe spot to keep my balance. *Calm, stay calm, just stay* calm. I glanced around, letting the others look for any sign of what had triggered the laser grid.

"Ah." Jackson had spotted something.

"Go on," the professor said.

"Red spots are pressure plates," Jackson explained. "We moved from one straight to another, didn't trip it. Must be a delayed sensor. Fail-safe somewhere?"

"There," the professor said, pausing the turn of my head. The deposit box's lock had a blinking LED next to its opening. "The actual key must need to be present to disable the grid."

"No way to crack it?"

"Not without a key."

"Well then," Henricks said. "Heather, I'm going to have to take over."

"What for?" I asked, alarmed. "And take over what?"

"Everything," Henricks replied, and suddenly my entire body was no longer my own, my consciousness pushed neatly aside as Henricks took the helm. I could see him flexing my fingers, twisting my wrists.

"What are you doing?" I asked. But Jackson was chuckling quietly.

"Haven't seen you do this for a while."

"And you won't," Henricks replied. "Not me, exactly, at any rate. Heather, sorry about this."

"What are you doing?"

"Why do you think I'm here?" he asked, stretching my legs carefully. "Not just to keep these two in line."

"Henricks here wasn't always a thief," the professor explained, trying and failing to hide his excitement. "He used to be an athlete. A gymnast, to be precise."

Henricks moved, and it was the most graceful thing my body had ever done.

He stepped over and under the laser beams neatly, delicately, twisting my limbs into poses I'd never thought possible. I did ballet when I was a kid, but this was levels above that. He twisted around another beam, then brought my leg up in a complex twist that neatly avoided another laser. I could feel the awe radiating from Jackson and the professor, felt my fair share myself, as Henricks artfully manoeuvred us towards the door. He whipped my long hair around a beam – my damn hair! – and ducked, the final set of beams in front of him. He stretched up on my pointed toes.

And I felt unbalanced, and just for a second I snatched back control out of panic, and Henricks stumbled and our foot just clipped the laser beam, and the alarms blared and Henricks just said "RUN!", so I did, bursting through the door and up towards the exit as fast as I could as we all heard the shouts of suddenly awake and vengeful guards echoing through the vault.

The greasy-haired suit sighs and sits back in his chair. He's not impressed with the version of the story I just told him, and I can't really blame him. I left out a lot of the important details, and changed some more besides. *The truth is for us alone.*

"Our neural scan did reveal that you had been scanned and prepared for remote mind-state projection and control."

"Yes."

"And you claim that this control was involuntary. That you were ... blank. Nothing but a vehicle for these men, Henricks, Jackson and Franz."

"Frank. But yeah, that's what happened."

"They kidnapped you, forcibly imprinted you for their Quarry, and then used you to carry out the theft."

"Yeah."

"And then abandoned you as you fled, once it was clear that you would not escape."

"That's right." That part was true. Only Jackson had apologised as I had felt the three piggybacking minds leave my own, closing the connection, leaving my body stumbling up the stairs to the sound of alarm bells. For what it was worth, his words had felt genuine. But that had been the deal all along – that was the whole point of using a Slate like me for a heist like this. *Deniability, for all parties. Real useful, isn't it?* The others didn't have their jewels, of course, and they'd have to lie low for a good while to avoid getting caught, but they'd made it out unscathed. And so would I.

I sit in silence, watching Shiny consult his notes, his brow furrowed. I knew what he was going to say, eventually. It had been done plenty of times before and would be again. The law and the courts hadn't caught up yet to this new tech, the possibility that criminals would hijack an unwilling body to commit their misdeeds. It had happened before, for certain, and the criminal underworld had swiftly taken advantage of the legal precedent set by the very high-profile case. Shiny couldn't prove that I had been in control, that Henricks, Jackson and the professor hadn't been driving my body the whole time. As far as the law was concerned, there was nothing he could do.

"Alright," Shiny says finally, and I suppress a smile. *At last.* "You're free to go. We will be contacting you for a further interview, and you may be required to issue a statement in court. We'll send you the paperwork."

"But I can leave?"

"You can leave." He scowls as he unlocks my cuffs and opens the door to the interview room. I smile at him broadly, and stroll up and out into the light of day, which hits my retinas like a searing fire. *But we're out. Free and clear.* Nobody had been hurt, except for a few bruises from when the guards had tackled me to the ground. Nobody was going to prison, unless Henricks and the gang got careless. Everything was fine. And, for some of us, it was better than fine. Much better.

You alright?

"Yeah," I mutter, trying not to move my lips too much; there were a lot of people on the street, and it was still considered weird to talk to yourself, even in this day and age. "You?"

Just fine. Home and comfortable.

"Did you check the transfer?"

All went through. Five hundred thousand, a little each from a dozen accounts.

"You're as good with computers as Frank."

Please. I can do things that would make him curl up and cry like a baby.

"I love you."

I love you too. Hurry back. This money's burning a hole in my pocket already.

"See you later."

See ya.

I feel her leave my mind: my constant companion, love of my life so far, sitting in our flat several miles away and unclipping the electrodes that had let her sit quietly in the back of my mind for days, through the initial meeting, the training, the set-up, and finally the heist itself. We'd planned it together – find some thieves with a heist ready and offer me as their Slate – she'd just handled a little extra computer work. If there could be four minds in one head, why not five? While they'd argued at the deposit box console, she'd taken over my hands and eyes for just long enough to do a little hacking of her own. The jewels were in the police evidence room, but five hundred thousand in ones and zeroes was sitting in our bank account, clamouring to be spent. It had only taken a minute, and we were comfortably rich. Though having her in the back of my mind had kept me sane, too. Had I been alone, I'd probably have shot myself just to shut Frank up.

I strolled down the street, grinning like an idiot, alone inside my head, but not in my heart.

Hûw Steer is an author, historian, and comedian from London. He has previously been published in The Future Fire's *Making Monsters* (2018), among other anthologies. His first novel, *The Blackbird and the Ghost*, was a semi-finalist in the 2019-20 Self-Published Fantasy Blog-Off. His second, *Ad Luna*, has just been released.

On this hot, busy night of the Center Flower's official bloom, the city's Board of Bloom Time Management blasts a star show in the square, injecting electric lights into the sky to demonstrate what a starlit night would look like. The perfect copper sidewalks, the wired streets, even the interconnected alleyways swarm with insects—

No, people. People gazing upward in awe, surrounded by electric versions of the Center Flower, waving fake lanterns that glow with the swish of a thumbprint. Buildings burn images in every window, flashing green, gold, pink, Spring, life, renewal. Children and parents meander through the festival-ridden streets, hailed by sweaty vendors. Some stand on porches with lanterns swinging. Everyone sings:

The Ghostlands

Bloom Time, Time of Blooms

And virtuous, joyous morning

(Or is the word mourning? a child at Swelter Park wonders, glancing at the ignited sky.)

The flowers with petals like tinkling bells,

They burst up from the ground.

And all the mothers look so pretty

In their new bright purple gowns.

The child, an eight-year-old girl with perpetually frizzy hair, hears the high whine of a mutt hunkering beneath a self-devouring dumpster. Something is wrong with the animal. His tail curls between his legs. He whimpers at the tendrils of man-made light sparking toward the sky.

The girl closes her eyes, reaching for the dog in the way Pap warns her not to. She's always had an odd brain, one with hyper-elastic electric signals, her neurons groping other nerve impulses nearby to feel what they feel.

The dog, she senses, fears something approaching, a wave of hot doom, a buildup of friction in the sky ... far away, a storm rolls and boils toward them, negatively charged clouds feeding off electrons that the city has accumulated over centuries.

The dog whines again.

"Pap," the girl whispers, dropping her lantern.

The storm devours the city for thirty-nine days, clawing and clashing, spitting high-voltage energy down on poles, wires, vehicles, people.

Across the city, household items explode: microwaves, televisions, washing machines, cooking mechanisms, bed heaters, chargeable books, electric instruments. Those connected to computer chips blast into fleshy debris when the chips detonate. Do not, the City Council advises over stuttering communication devices addressed to the city, connect yourself to a computer chip at this time. Do not turn on any appliances. Electric Usage CO, a cluster of copper buildings in the City Center, explodes, sending the death count into thousands.

Mariah Montoya

A stink of rotting meat permeates the air.

The frizzy-haired girl cowers inside with Pap and her grandmother, who caresses her antique, non-electric rocking chair with petunias printed on its fabric.

"Clarice," Pap murmurs constantly, "I must take you and Gran to Charpelle."

"Charpelle, Pap," the girl repeats. Charpelle, the city in the west, where it's rumored the storm isn't so bad. But vehicles are dangerous now: their generators entice lightning when activated. So they stay, resisting the electric pollution that strangles them with fingers of invisible hot wire. Clarice tries to push the pollution off Pap and Gran with her brain's throbbing pulses, but soon the air singes their skin. Blisters blossom on their necks.

Outside, beetle-like people flee their homes, scuttling through the streets with scorched faces, carrying possessions or children. Charpelle, they shout, head to Charpelle! They follow the railroad tracks, ancient rusted metal that the city kept as a memorial to honor the days before plugs and wires and screens.

Soon, despite Pap's frantic protests, Gran hobbles from the condo in delirium, tugging along her flower-patterned rocking chair. When her burned, bony arms grow exhausted, she leaves the rocking chair by the railroad, kissing its mahogany handles goodbye. Clarice senses Gran's brain activity cease not long afterward.

Bloom Time, Time of Blooms, some sing as they squat in their homes, accepting death. The song wafts through walls and reaches Clarice, who, understanding the storm in a way no one else does, refuses to sing along.

Her electric heartbeat knows the storm will not relent until it has proven that power from human hands is nothing compared to power from the sky.

Half-demolished buildings sit cold, lifeless, black. Vehicles scatter the city like dismembered body parts. Real bodies rot, nibbled by roaches that survived. Above the destroyed Electric Usage CO, a swirl of clouds still boils, angry and black, sputtering lightning, sending reverberations throughout the skeleton of the city.

Shattered glass litters the streets, glistening like fallen stars.

Clarice, sprawled beside her foul-smelling, blackened father, eventually devours the last of the canned goods, licking bean starch off her fingers. She leaves Pap's carcass behind, picking her way through the rubbish in the streets. Her hair floats skyward now, but it seems the electricity cannot otherwise touch her; some protective shield clings to her body, as if her neurons fought back and deflected the pollution that killed everyone else.

"The dog," Clarice says out loud, to nobody. "I hope the dog's alive." Then the ghost of Pap's voice floods her: Charpelle.

Near dusk, she makes it to the railroad tracks near Gedderum Street, where gray clouds hover hesitantly overhead like mothballs. A familiar flower-patterned rocking chair sits upright by the tracks, creaking slightly as it rocks in the wind.

Clarice sinks into it, her mind on food, willing a rodent to scurry across her feet.

A rat does so, dashing from beneath a pile of rubble. With utmost concentration, she funnels electricity toward it, zapping the creature with a temperature that cooks. She peels back its fur and eats. She sings for Pap, her throat thick, sticky, and moist:

The flowers with petals like tinkling bells,

They burst up from the ground.

And all the mothers look so pretty

In their new bright purple gowns.

It's strangely cool in these Ghostlands, as if the storm swept away all that stifling heat. Clarice will trail the tracks in the morning, but for now she snuggles into Gran's rocking chair. The destruction around her is illuminated by something peering through the fading clouds. Something she has only ever seen in pictures on screens. Something that has, until now, been smothered by smog and outshined by electricity since before Clarice was born:

A single star beams upon a city that hasn't felt true starlight in two hundred years.

Mariah Montoya is a writer from Idaho, the United States. Her short stories have been published in *Metaphorosis, Typehouse Literary Magazine, Jersey Devil Press*, and others. Her Middle Grade chapter book, *The Very Secret Door In Classroom 19*, is available on Amazon.
Besides writing, Mariah loves exercising and teaching dance.

A Cracked Teapot

Sherry Shahan

I ris longs to be with others who resist State laws; others who risk punishment to express themselves however they choose; others who believe that what a person dreams is more important than exams devised to test how little you know about history. She's been searching for a group she heard about during a blackout: C.R.A.P. The Criminally Rebellious Adolescent Population supposedly live in a crumbling 20th-century bomb shelter, playing instruments ripped off from the State Repository: assorted brass and drums, a piano with non-synthetic keys.

Iris dreams of joining them.

She risks venturing above ground, hunkering over the rusty handlebars of a felonious ten-speed, pedaling above the transit tube that links one underground metropolis to the next, sweating inside her black neoprene wetsuit, black skullcap, black combat boots, hoping all her blackness will blend into the inky night. A guitar is slung over her shoulder.

Up here, in the messed-up ozone, all is as quiet as the day personal transport became illegal. Everyone knows people once lived above ground, drove vehicles with built-in music systems, and made babies in the backseat instead of in petri dishes.

That was before the last trumped-up election.

Iris immerses herself in a new theory, letting it expand from conjecture to verity. What if State-professed enemies are imaginary? Who would know in a world where lies are passed off as truths and truth is virtually unknown?

She wonders why the old and diseased don't rise from beneath the State's tyrannical thumb. Break into the Repository and steal bikes, skateboards, scooters, wheelchairs – anything to propel them down an unbroken path to freedom. What do they have to lose?

Her boots beat the pedals, wheels spinning as a drone spirals toward her. If it detects her neuro-waves, her whereabouts will be transmitted to the State lickety-split. Those who violate curfew disappear for good.

She chokes the handlebars, praying the metal frame will interfere with the eye-beam, deflecting rays like a shield. The drone moves swiftly, sputtering overhead, *"We're watching you C.R.A.P. You're never out of our sight."*

Iris ducks as sparks ricochet off the bike rims and singe her wetsuit. The drone oscillates strangely before dropping and exploding.

The bike protected her!

She pedals back to her zone, a lone figure among fleshy rats with gray, expressionless faces. Tomorrow night she'll venture further, intent on finding C.R.A.P., now certain they exist. Otherwise, why program a drone with the C.R.A.P. message?

Iris pauses near the opening of her underground unit, a metal tunnel that leads to an equally rigid life-pod. She turns, hearing the unmistakable melody of a human voice. Who would risk defying the curfew ordinance?

She dares to ask, "Anyone there?"

No answer.

Iris swings off her bike, works the front wheel into rubble, ignoring the hum of diagnetics below. "It's okay," she says. "I'm C.R.A.P. Like *certifiably.*"

She senses movement, shuffles closer, and raises two fingers in a primitive peace sign. "Hello?"

Then Iris sees her. A girl about sixteen, lying on her back, arms crossed over her chest. What shocks Iris most is the neglect of her uniform, which sends a message to the State – *"up yours"* – a phrase she'd learned in her *History is Fiction* class.

The girl caresses a pet rat.

Iris smiles, believing in goodness. "What're you doing up here?"

The girl moans.

"Are you okay?" Iris kneels by her side. Finely spun hair frames the most exquisite face. But her eyes are vitreous. Iris has seen that expression before; but she isn't sure if it's hope or fear.

The girl's unruly presence gives her courage. "Are you C.R.A.P.?"

The girl moans again and sinks further into herself.

Iris wonders if being C.R.A.P. means you're a little bit crazy. If allowing yourself to *feel*, like the State says, is the definition of madness.

She swings her guitar around and plays a few chords.

The girl begins to sob.

"Please, don't cry." If only Iris had learned to sing – but when she relaxes her throat, a discordant quaver seeps out.

The girl sobs louder. "It's just so … so beautiful."

Iris sets her guitar aside. "Where did you come from?"

"Petri-X." The girl sounds ashamed.

Iris stares at the curve of her neck. Perfect, unflawed. She's removed her surgically implanted auditory-phone. Wires dangle daintily from her ear. Iris disconnected her own phone the last time she sneaked out.

Iris would purr her name if she knew it. "I've never met another C.R.A.P."

The girl's eyelids flutter. "I hear there are more like us. Up here, hiding in ancient restaurants and prehistoric strip malls." She moves her arms, revealing a tear in the front of her uniform where she'd severed her feeding tube.

"Are you hungry?" Iris asks. The girl appears starved.

She nods. "I'm Lily."

Iris lifts the top half of her wetsuit and unwinds her feeding line. It swells like a tiny inner tube. She licks the end before inserting it through the tear in Lily's uniform, gently working it into her navel clamp, allowing her own life juices to flow into Lily.

Lily scans the wetsuit. "You look like a victim of pyrotechnics."

Iris hiccups.

Iris and Lily meet like this each night in the mangled milieu of glass, steel, and concrete that was once museums, libraries, hair salons, and video arcades.

Iris plays guitar. Lily paints, using the old-world technique of fresco. Tons of plaster litter the ground, so no problem there.

Iris watches Lily separate areas of her canvas with a flat piece of metal and sketch sensual curves of landscapes on the rough surfaces. Scenes of fertile fields and swelling seas, bucolic places they'll never see or smell.

Lily lulls Iris with tales of paintbrushes woven from her hair and tints mixed from tears. "I tried State-sanctioned art," Lily says with a lazy stroke, adding carmine to an otherwise colorless world. "We were required to replicate the classics from archaic books. Mine were exact copies, garnering approval and favor, but I was nothing but a serf. Crippled inside."

"So you ran away?"

"Do you believe we have mothers, fathers, sisters, or brothers other than those in the lab?" Lily asks, chewing the end of her brush. "I once dreamed of being excavated from the belly of a wailing woman."

"I had a similar dream."

"They only want us to know what they want us to know." Lily resumes painting. "I prefer High Renaissance art to 20th-century soup cans. Don't you?"

"Uh, sure."

"I once tore at my flesh as a way to call myself back from nothingness."

Iris gasps a little. "It's up to us to create the light."

Lily cradles her pet rat and lets it perch on her shoulder. His pink tail skims the hollow between Lily's breasts. Iris has to look away.

"Imagine spending four years lying on your back painting a ceiling," Lily says. "So long ago, yet his images tell the history of creation and the fall of humanity. Did you know Michelangelo wrote sonnets before Shakespeare?"

She recites:

I feel as lit by fire a cold countenance
That burns me from afar...
I feel two shapely arms...
Without motion moves every balance.

"Where did you learn that?" Iris asks.

"Elder Abraham."

Iris marvels at the way great thoughts seep from Lily's mind. "I'll set it to music."

"We can't keep meeting here," Lily says, her voice no longer frail, gaining strength from the nightly injections. "We need a place that's ours alone."

The universe had dropped perfect C.R.A.P. in her junk pile. They even have the same thoughts at the same time. Like all star-crossed lovers.

Luxurious nights pass in secrecy above ground.

Lily grinds plaster and mixes pigment in preparation for their journey. "Being together like this is pure light," she says. "They can't lock up our hearts."

Iris tunes her guitar to Lily's breath. The frequency lifts her for any uncertainties ahead. She packs essentials: antiseptic swabs to clean her feeding tube and the box of Super Strike Bowling Alley matches she unearthed, worth a fortune on the black market. A corroded hubcap becomes a second bike seat.

When it's time to set off, Iris slips the top half of her extra wetsuit over Lily's ragged uniform. "To blend with the darkness."

"If only..." Lily stops.

Iris understands completely. No one can be wholly beautiful in State-issued shoes. Guaranteed *ugly* for life. She steps from her boots. "Wear these."

Lily smiles, lovely as a cellulose rose.

They travel under a moonless sky. No stars. No asteroids. Only dust particles and chemical pollutants extending into the atmosphere. They pass an enormous billboard: *Fear the Enemy. Deport. Deport. Deport.*

"Can we really survive on our own?" Lily keeps asking. "Find a place away from spies who are so wicked and sleepless?"

"We'll discover one," Iris says.

"It's a dream waiting to happen."

Iris wants to say something equally brilliant, if only she had the words. But then, a conversation wasn't really necessary when two lovers agreed. No one had ever been so in tune with her, not even her petri-parents. Sure, they'll miss her, as she'll miss them. No doubt they'll spawn a clone from her DNA, without the recessive C.R.A.P. gene.

Her diagnosis had come in Institutional Day Care when her brain rejected the requisite digital chip. A month of interface examinations revealed a hypersensitivity to mandated directives. Her QR tattoo scans *social, emotional, damaged.*

On the seventh day of their trek, Iris and Lily settle in the bowels of a toppled theme park, in a moat where the head of a decapitated Alice-in-Wonderland lolls in a cracked teacup. They stow away during the day, foraging at night for anything useful – hauling off smashed, broken bits of this and that.

A miniature castle door becomes their front gate. They plant a plastic palm, add a garden flamingo. Scraps of wire mesh are woven into a dome roof in the hope of protecting them from drone rays.

Michelangelo eliminates marauding rats, pulverizing spines and skulls, growing fat as a fabled cow. Lily tans the hides, stitches them together, and fabricates something called wall-to-wall carpet.

Iris works to curve a splintered wooden stake into a bow. She braids twine, knots it over the ends, pulls it taut. Another stake becomes an arrow with a razor-sharp point. Lily fashions an over-the-shoulder sleeve from hides.

Meanwhile, they're in dire need of a tube feeding.

Iris rummages around, uncovering a case of Cool Ranch Doritos, which had somehow survived the expiration date. "A feast!"

"Illustrious!" Lily presses her lips to Iris's mouth; Iris loses herself in a primeval memory of vanilla and orange blossoms.

"Ours is the happiest place on earth," Lily says.

Iris picks up her guitar, arranging words in an elaborate language.

Lily works pigment into wet plaster, languishing over her latest fresco, *Iris's Song*. Michelangelo nibbles her toe.

Iris shoos him away. "Doesn't that hurt?"

Lily seems oblivious. "What, my sweet?"

"Your toe," Iris says. "It's bleeding."

"Red! Quick! Fetch a receptacle!"

Soon the trees in *Iris's Song* bloom scarlet.

Iris never hungered for her more.

They no longer talk about searching for other C.R.A.P.

Early one morning, Lily weeps over something she can't explain. Iris believes her tears are opalescent from the absorption of fluids through the feeding tube. It must have extra nutrients, she reasons, because Lily's breasts are overflowing with the same milky substance.

Lily fashions a tent-like dress for herself. *"Rock-a-bye, baby, on the tree top."*

Iris doesn't know if it's a song or a poem or how she knows the next line, *"When the wind blows, the cradle will rock."*

Summer heat rages and violent winds consume the crumbling ruins, sweeping away Lily's last morsel of plaster. She cries and cries, her tears raining on seething thermals.

Iris repairs a broken-down cart for a trek outward. "I'll gather enough plaster to last forever after."

"When we're together I'm rarely afraid," Lily says. Her beautiful eyes gather Iris in and then cast her off. "Promise you'll come back…"

"Your heart will travel with me."

Iris shoulders her sheath, places the bow in the cart, and pushes it into a twilight strange with colors. It's as if someone sprayed everything gunmetal gray. She thinks about her life with Lily; how she creates art from nothing, knowing no one but Iris will see it. Just as Iris shapes songs, knowing no one but Lily will hear them.

She worries about Lily's swollen belly, fearing it may be an invasive growth. Instead of looking for plaster she should be whisking Lily underground to a clinic. But that would mean turning themselves in to the State. They'd be put on display, sealed in separate glass cubicles. Separated, forever.

The windstorm slowly dies.

Iris wheels the cart around debris, pausing near a pyramid of ash where a mischief of rats groom themselves. All wear collars.

"Domesticated!"

The implications leave her breathless. *Pets? Or spies?* Impossible to know.

A mangy rat skulks forward, staring through soulless eyes. Iris grips her bow, retrieves the arrow, and fires. The arrow is a winged creature, flying smoothly and taking the rodent by surprise. She recovers the bloody shaft and leaves the rat to the others.

Further on, Iris exhumes a chunk of moldy stucco – a thrilling moment since Lily doesn't have that shade of green. She leverages the stucco into the cart beside the bow and visualizes Lily's impish glee. Even in a wetsuit Iris feels sticky leakage from her tube.

The day's last light shakes a dusty haze.

Closer to the moat, an unfamiliar scent assaults her. Sweet and salty. But not unpleasant. The fragrance lulls her, pulls her the rest of the way home.

Michelangelo hunches by the gate; ichor stains his whiskers.

Iris rushes by him, seeing her lovely reclining and naked, a primitive portrait. "Lily!"

Lily smiles, cradling a writhing bundle.

It lets out a wail, a cacophony of hope and promise.

Iris kneels beside her family and serenades them with song.

Sherry Shahan lives in a laid-back beach town in California where she grows carrot tops in ice cube trays for pesto. Her writing has appeared in Oxford University Press, Los Angeles Times, Exposition Review, Confrontation and forthcoming from Gargoyle and F(r)iction. She holds an MFA from Vermont College of Fine Arts.

The Cyclops

Teika Marija Smits

23rd March

Had another day of tests yesterday. I don't feel like writing after a day of being prodded and poked. The tests they make me do and the tests they perform *on* me, to gauge the state of my immune health, seem to go on forever. It's exhausting.

Ten weeks ago, before the accident, when I was still a house officer at one of the busiest hospitals in London I was too busy to go on a date. Too busy to phone my mother. Too busy to write in a sodding diary. If *I'd* had *me* as a patient I'd have been intrigued. I'd have wanted to see the eye.

Of course they want to prod and poke me.

24th March

More emails today. Loads from those awful people who claim they can see angels and auras. I'm deleting them. Surely they've read in the papers that I'm a doctor – correction: *was a doctor* – and not into woo.

I still can't get my head around the fact that I'm never going to do my rounds again. The whole six-months-to-live thing is probably what I should be thinking about, but I'm not. I keep thinking about work and its small joys: the patients who make me smile despite myself; drinking coffee with Luke and gossiping about our line manager; planning our trip to Namibia.

I'd always hated what I looked like before I went to the country of my mother's people. Growing up in the 90s, in Surrey, and being one of only a handful of girls who didn't have pink skin was pretty shit. Mind you, it never did my mum any harm – I mean, being the beautiful, black outsider. She was the model of the moment in the 80s. Then she met my dad. My screwed-up American dad who was the photographer of the moment.

When Mum found out she was pregnant with me I guess he thought that the moment was over. He stuck around long enough to make sure I was delivered safe and sound, but when he actually had to do stuff, dad stuff, he disappeared into his work. But now he's interested in his miraculous daughter. He actually phoned the other day.

In Namibia I didn't stick out like a sore thumb. It felt good to be amongst women who looked like me; I saw myself in their faces. And their high cheekbones, wide mouths and large brown eyes reminded me that beauty – normalcy – is all about context.

Luke had tried to rile me by saying that now *he* was the exotic doctor surrounded by all these beautiful women I'd have to watch out.

I laughed and then reminded him that as soon as we were back in London he'd be desperately in love with me again – yet still too busy with work to actually go on a date.

He keeps calling me, inviting himself round, but I've been ignoring him. I don't want to look into his eyes again; to see all those magnificent colours – all those wavelengths of invisible light – the colours of horror and pity and fascination, and worst of all, grief in abeyance.

25th March

More emails and phone calls. The call from the MoD was particularly scary. They've invited me over to discuss my "particularly keen" vision; to see if I can help them with their "defence strategies". Not bloody likely. It's because of "defence" organisations like them that I've only got six months to live. Actually, it's five months now. I said no to their offer.

Journalists have been pestering me to give them an exclusive. I've told them no again and again. I unplugged the phone earlier this evening and was glad of the silence. My smartphone's been turned off for ages already. I can't do much about the idiots waiting outside my flat but I figure they'll get called out to other stories at some point soon.

Mum's asked me to come home, which might give me some peace from the journos, but I'm not sure I want to. I've got pretty much everything I need right here; my books, some food (not that I feel like eating much) and best of all, the skylight above my bed. I spend a lot of my time simply gazing up at the sky.

My telescopic vision is improving day by day. The nanobots, or whatever the hell they are, never seem to let up. They really are building me a magnificent eye. It's like having a light microscope, the Hubble telescope and an infra-red camera, and whatever, all rolled into one, slap bang in the middle of my forehead. Though it's a pity that the nanobots are shredding my immune system.

26th March

Last night I dreamt about the accident again. Luke and I have just finished our day's work at Rundu Hospital and Kagiso asks us if we want to see the place where the shooting star landed. We agree and then get into Kagiso's truck and on to God-only-knows where. And then we're out of the truck and walking across barren earth and into a crater about the size of a netball field. There isn't much to see – the meteorite is just a blackened boulder. Though when it's struck by the light from the setting sun it sparkles as though it's alive with thousands of miniature fireflies. Kagiso and I touch it and a shard of black crust comes away in my hand. And then Kagiso is distracted by something. He runs; away from the meteorite, out of the crater and out across the dry earth, pointing and shouting at the sky. And then I see it too – the comet – and I begin to run as well, the shard still in my hand, and somehow tingling. Luke's yelling at us to come back; he says it might not be safe out there, but I can't stop running. I've got to see the shooting star land. Kagiso's a hell of a runner and I can't keep up with him, so I slow and stop and try to catch my breath. Then the landmine explodes. In one roiling instant, Kagiso is torn to bits and fear shears through me as I realize that there's no way I can escape the flying metal and rock that is about to slice through my skull and into my eyes, taking away my sight as I used to know it. And that's always when I wake up, drenched in sweat, and fighting for breath.

27th March

Mum came over today. She forced her way through the journos outside and yelled up at the window for me to buzz her in. She's subtle like that.

I couldn't help but notice her shudder when she looked at me as I opened the door to the flat. Correction, when she saw *the eye*. But then she hugged me and started to cry. Typically, she told me off for making her worried sick by not answering her calls.

She plugged the phone in; said she'd been trying to get hold of me for days. At first, I was pissed off with her for having a go at me. After all, I've got a right to decide how I'm going to spend the next five months of my life, but she's having none of it. Says she's going to stay with me from now on: to look after me and talk about my options. My treatment. I told her that conventional treatment wouldn't do a thing. But she ignored me and went on about me taking the immunosuppressants that some of the medics think would help. *Then* she started baking cheese muffins, breaking off to field phone calls for me. At six o'clock she unplugged the phone and poured herself a large glass of wine. *Darling,* she said (I hate it when she calls me darling – I know that something unpleasant is coming next) *do you have any idea of what is going on in your body?* I sighed, my real – though useless – eyes prickling with tears that would never come, and told her that no, I didn't know what was going on. Only that, somehow, I knew that the nanobots, whatever, weren't malicious. But they were nosy, all right. I felt as though I was seeing the world through the eyes (okay, eye) of someone else. And that everything was new and strange, and well … of interest.

Later, she cooked us a huge bowl of spaghetti bolognese and then we watched a film. It was the first time in ages I actually enjoyed eating something.

28th March

As I was checking my emails today (there were loads from Luke) Mum took a phone call from a Professor at MIT. She passed me the phone and said that I needed to speak to him since he's the leading expert in nanotechnology.

So… we're now booked on the next flight to Boston. Mum's packing our bags as I write this.

I've gotta go now. She's asking me how many knickers I want to take. Jesus.

5th April

So the whole flight thing – trying to get through the airport unnoticed by the press and unaffected by all the germs out there – was a nightmare. I still managed to catch a cold with all the precautions we took and of course it's not shifting. I had half-expected to see Luke at the airport; I thought Mum would tell him that we were going – she's always going on about him being my saviour because he was the one, mostly unhurt by the landmine, who got me back to the hospital and arranged for me to be flown back to the UK. But it seems that she took my "don't call Luke" requests seriously.

Life here is weird. They're taking blood from me almost daily and performing dozens of tests on it. They reckon that if they can just figure out how the nanobots work they can somehow neutralize them. But the bots are like nothing they've ever seen before. It's ironic really – the fact that I, with my weakened immune system, have flown all the way across the Atlantic (catching a cold in the process) just to have them say this to me, because I could have told them that. The nanobots have built my incredible eye, which can focus in on Venus on a clear day, so of course they'd be out-of-this world amazing.

12th April

We keep going around in circles when it comes to the question of immunosuppressants. Some of the team say we should try them; that they'll dampen my immune system and so stop it from attacking the nanobots. And then *that* might make the nanobots stop killing off my immune system. Others disagree. But as I've got a cold already, I don't think it would be a good idea. The team are still baffled by the nanobots, and nothing that they've tried on them, to destroy them, has worked. So this cold's probably going to kill me.

When I'm not in the lab, I spend most of my time in bed or outside, looking at the night sky. I don't have a good view of the sky from my room so Mum takes me out in a wheelchair and wraps me in blankets so that I can gaze at the stars, which are incredible. She brings me hot chocolate and tries not to cry. I wish I could cry, but I can't. Along with the destruction of my old eyes – my real eyes – my tear ducts were damaged in the blast and my new eye, the imposter, has no need of them. I guess that spectacularly clever nanobots do not cry.

20th April

The Professor's latest idea is to hook me up to some software so that the team can see what I see. They reckon that if they can "interface" with the eye, where the nanobots are still busy, they can learn more about them. So I'll roll with this, whatever, although I know that this is just about them being nosy. I think it might be good to have someone else see what I see.

21st April

Today was super-weird. I mean, I was expecting it to be strange to have the team see what I see, but on a screen, but it was still really weird. They went silent when I showed them how good my microscopic vision was by focussing in on the scar tissue around my hand where the sharp crust of Kagiso's meteorite scratched me when I was hit by the landmine. I – and they – looked at the individual cells and watched the odd nanobot (microbot, I guess?) cruising through the scar tissue, still on patrol. They'd already hypothesized that this must have been one of the ways that the nanobots entered my body, going on to try to fix my severed optical nerves, but still, it was good to see the evidence for this hypothesis. I noticed a couple of them whispering, once again distracted by the *what and how and why* of a meteorite covered in nanobots, something I'd often considered myself, but the Professor soon silenced them.

Another weird thing though, that they, and I, can't quite figure out is why I'm not infectious. I mean, back in London, they were super-precautious, assuming that whatever was building my eye and wrecking my immune system would be contagious, but for some reason, the nanobots aren't interested in anyone else. They're sticking to me, and me only. Which is a relief, I guess. At least I don't feel guilty about anyone else having to go through what I'm going through. But of course I can't help but ask, why? Why me? Why did it have to be me?

Then came the instructions from the research team, dressed up as polite requests. So many of them. Could I look at this object, please, and view it in ultraviolet? Could I now look at them all in infra-red? And then could I go outside and focus in on the moon? I was exhausted by it all, and glad when it was over and back in my room.

Mum looked at me funny when she helped me into bed and I had to explain why I now have what looks like a memory stick attached to the left side of my head where the shrapnel from the landmine sliced through my skull and into the back of my eyes. *They're spying on me, on what the eye can see,* I said. She didn't look happy about that at all and went off on a long rant about privacy and consent. Stuff that she thinks she's the expert on, because of her modelling days. I had to explain that it's not always on and that *I'm* the one who gets to decide when they do their spying. She seemed okay about that and then changed the subject, asking, again, if I'd thought about contacting Luke. I told her no, in my firm, but exasperated voice, that I did not want to put Luke through the anguish of being with someone about to die. And I didn't want him to see me like this.

24th April

When I went into the lab today there was a really strange atmosphere. The Professor looked nervous and said that, if I didn't mind, there'd be a few people coming round today to have a look at what my eye could see. I told him that I guessed he was no closer to a cure. He shifted his weight and said that, no, he wasn't any closer to disabling the nanobots. The more they learnt about them, the more they discovered about their complexity. Which is why he wanted some experts, and *relevant others*, to look at me.

I said it would be okay, (I'm pretty much resigned to being the world's number one freak show at the moment) but only on the condition that they didn't try to recruit me or anything.

So various people came and went, requesting me to look at this and that. Most of them treated me like a robot, but the guy from NASA was kind. He wheeled me outside, as the sun was setting, and brought me hot chocolate, topped with whipped cream. He talked to me about the constellations, and the Greeks who had named many of them, and how Gaia was the mother of the three Cyclops in Greek mythology. *This* was news to me, and when I joked to Mum later on that she must have seen into the future, or something, when she'd named me, she went all huffy and proceeded to remind me that Gaia was also Mother Earth. And *that* was why I'd been given that name; because she loved me more than the Earth itself. She had a good cry then and as usual I ended up feeling bad for upsetting her.

27th April

So I joked to the team today that rather than investigating the nanobots, it was time, maybe, that they thought about granting me my dying wish. They looked embarrassed then, because I'd acknowledged their failure, and finally the Professor said that he was sorry, and yes, he would like to know what my dying wish was. I don't know why I said it, but I thought about the night sky, and I said that I'd like to see all that there was to see of the universe. His face went all weird then, and he looked at me with an expression I couldn't quite read. But then, strangely, he smiled. He said that he was sure that Robert (the guy from NASA) would love to help. When he'd seen what my eye could see he was, apparently, very keen to persuade me to work with him, saying that if I wasn't stuck here on Earth the things I could see would be mind-blowing. It could answer many of their unanswered questions. But the Professor hadn't told me, you know, because of the whole "no recruiting thing". So, anyway, I'm going to speak to Robert again tomorrow.

28th April

I am going into space! OH MY GOD!

29ᵗʰ April

Mum's completely freaking out about the whole going-into-space thing, but she also knows that NASA want me to go and that I'm dead set on going. The Professor had a word with her and broke it to her that he couldn't do any more for me, so I may as well go into space, and be of use. *But what about me?* she kept asking, over and over, and the poor guy had to comfort her somehow.

So ... I've been signing away my last vestiges of privacy to SpaceX, who are going to work alongside NASA, so that I can get on a commercial space rocket as soon as possible and go to the International Space Station. Once I'm up there, I'm going to be linked up to the Station's computer and I'll be broadcasting what I can see to the whole world. Oh, and they want me to vlog. So in a few days I'll be leaving for Cape Canaveral to meet the crew of the rocket, and to learn a few of the basics of space flight. (Although it's obvious that I'm the human equivalent of Laika in this situation they still want me to learn enough so that I don't do anything stupid out there.) I cannot even begin to explain how happy I am right now.

30ᵗʰ April

I don't know whether it's because of my happier mood, but I felt much better today. Less snotty, and as though some energy was returning to me. Of course I can't possibly hope to cram in what would usually be two years' worth of astronaut training into a fortnight, but at least I'll learn enough so I won't be a liability.

1ˢᵗ May

I went to see the Professor's team today, to say my goodbyes, and although I'd been half-expecting this to happen, when it did, it freaked me out. There, in the lab, was Kagiso's meteorite, glittering like a bastard. With Luke standing next to it.

14ᵗʰ May

These past two weeks have been beyond strange. Exhausting, exhilarating, heartbreaking, and confusing. Turns out I was wrong about Luke. There is nothing but the infra-red of love in his eyes and we've spent every minute together when I haven't been doing my preparations with the crew. Mum's been in tears most of the fortnight and when Dad came to see me, she asked him to stay with her.

I should be worried about going into space, but I'm not. The one thing that's been worrying me has been the prospect of them *not* letting me go. I'm absolutely desperate to get out there, but because of something the Professor said to me before I left MIT I've been certain that any minute the whole thing would be cancelled.

You're transmitting, he'd said, his voice low. He had to repeat himself, because I didn't respond. I was too ... freaked out to respond. He went on to explain that he was only telling me now, because only now was he sure. I (or the eye, or the nanobots, whatever) had been transmitting a message, and although he'd noticed something when I'd first been hooked up to the computer, it had taken him a while to realize what it meant. I asked him what the message was. *SOS*, he said.

Transcript of Video Diary: 15ᵗʰ May 18.02 UTC

>> GAIA: Um, okay, so this is weird. I mean, this whole vlog thing is weird, but blasting off the Earth and to *here*, to the space station, is weird. Saying goodbye to my mum and dad and Luke

[blows nose]

was weird. And today I slept, ate some of the packaged food Kirsty and Dmitri promised me I'll get accustomed to and then I looked upon the Eye of God, otherwise known as the Helix Nebula. To see the solar winds roaring through the "iris", where the star used to exist is just, well…

[coughs]

I'm pretty exhausted actually so um, I'm just gonna sleep now.

Transcript of Video Diary: 16th May 18.05 UTC

>>GAIA: Hi everyone. So from today's footage you'll see that I've been focussing on the Pillars of Creation in the Eagle Nebula – the place where stars are born out of hydrogen. There's already a fair bit of information about them but I was drawn to them because I've seen the Hubble photos, and they're just amazing. But being here, and seeing them, was just…

[coughs]

incredible. I managed to get an even higher resolution image to what had gone before, so that was cool. What I find poignant about them is the fact that they don't actually exist – I mean, as we see them in pictures now. The light is taking ages to reach us because they're thousands of light years away. Kirsty told me that a supernova near them exploded and, poof, they were all blown to smithereens. I mean, how sad is that? Apparently, it'll take another thousand years for us to see what's left of the pillars. Okay, well, I've really got to sleep now. Night all.

Transcript of Video Diary: 17th May 18.01 UTC

>>GAIA:

[sniffs]

So I thought I felt rough because of the space travel, but it's not wearing off. Kirsty and Dmitri, here with me in the quarantine section, have been great, making sure I'm well looked after, but I'm pretty sure the cold is now flu. My temperature is literally sky high and my muscles ache so bad. So I haven't got long. But, hey, in other news, something that I saw today got the guys from NASA super-excited. I managed to (and this makes little sense to me, by the way)

[coughs]

but I managed to detect some baryonic dark matter within a brown dwarf, which is a kind of lesser star that, funnily enough, to the human eye would look fuchsia – you know, that horrid shade of pink that was so fashionable in the 1980s. That stuff is difficult to see, apparently, but I did it. They've been asking me about the non-baryonic dark matter (the stuff that isn't made of protons and neutrons and impossible to see because it doesn't give out any kind of electromagnetic radiation) but I'm not sure how I'm supposed to find something that's invisible. It made me think of you, Luke, when I asked you what I should look for when I got out here. You told me that I should look at the beautiful stuff (I have, but there's a hell of a lot of that) and you also said that I should look at the nondescript stuff too, because interesting stuff was happening there as well. But how can I see what can't be seen?

[sneezes]

Okay. Sorry folks, that's all I can manage today.

Transcript of Video Diary: 18th May 18.06 UTC

So as you've probably seen from today's footage, there are two, habitable-looking planets in one of Andromeda's satellite galaxies. And a weird-looking rocket (or would that be spaceship?) on the edge of our solar system, that has so far gone undetected. It's travelling towards us. Fast. The astronauts are (and very nearly literally) over the moon about it. They're saying it's confirmation of alien life.

[sniffs]

I'd really like to be able to look for gravitational waves, like some of the scientists from LIGO suggested I do, but I'm sorry, I need to sleep.

[cries]

I would like to sleep forever.

Transcript of Video Diary: 19th May 18:03 UTC

>> GAIA: My muscles won't stop shaking. I can't stand it. The pain is…

[sobs]

This might be the last time I can do this, so I just wanted to say a few things.

[sniffs]

Mum, thanks for raising me pretty much single-handedly. You did an amazing job. I love you. And Dad, I know you love me, really. And I love you too. Luke, I'm sorry. I should have made more time for you. If we'd had kids, maybe their great-grandchildren's great-grandchildren may have been around to witness the sight of the crumbling Pillars of Creation. Or maybe they'd be learning about the composition of dark matter in their physics lessons. Or studying to become doctors. I don't know. But I do know that I love you.

Transcript of Video Diary: 19th May 21:19 UTC

>> GAIA: I've plugged myself in again. I thought, what the hell? It's up to you guys to decide whether you want to see what death looks like to me. Who knows, the footage may prove useful. And I'm going to leave the camera running while I lie here and gaze out at the stars. Kirsty's going to sit with me.

Transcript of Video Diary: 19th May 23.49 UTC

>> GAIA: Kirsty?

>> KIRSTY: Yes?

>> GAIA: D'you think we'll ever know what dark matter is made of?

>> KIRSTY: I don't know. Probably not any time soon.

>> GAIA: It's around us all the time, though, isn't it? We just can't see it.

>> KIRSTY: Yes. But we can see its effects. There's evidence for its existence.

>> GAIA: A bit like love. We can't see it, but we know it's there because of what it makes us do.

>> KIRSTY: Yes. Yes, that's right.

>> GAIA: [sighs] Or we don't notice it until it's too late. Like life. We don't notice its beauty until it's too late.

[silence]

>> GAIA: Kirsty?

>> KIRSTY: Yes?

>> GAIA: I'm scared.

>> KIRSTY: It's okay, Gaia. It'll be okay.

[silence]

[Door opens]

>> DMITRI: Kirsty? Is Gaia? I mean, how's she doing?

>> KIRSTY: I think she's … just left us.

[checks Gaia's pulse]

>> KIRSTY: Oh God, yes.

[takes a deep breath]

>> KIRSTY: But the eye – it's still moving. I don't understand. It seems to be focussing and re-focussing. Why is it doing that?

>> DMITRI: Kirsty, we just got a message. An extra-terrestrial message. In binary. The other crew members have been translating it.

>> KIRSTY: And?

>> DMITRI: It says, *We have received your message and we are sorry that you are hurt. We did not intend for our spies to do damage; they do not know enough about your physiology, Mother-Cyclops. But we will undo the damage. Wait, and all will be well. We are coming for you.*

Teika Marija Smits is a Nottingham-based writer, editor and mother-of-two. Her speculative fiction has appeared in various places including Reckoning, Theaker's Quarterly Fiction and Best of British Science Fiction 2018. In spare moments she likes to doodle. https://marijasmits.wordpress.com/ @MarijaSmits

We Fall Like Leaves Fall

Raman Mundair

White-Out // //

In time they would speak of the white-out days as having consumed them alive. The forced orbit around whiteness had to be corrected. Its unbalance impacted on all hues. But of course the darker melanated women suffered the most. Sleep cycles were out of sync. Deep rest was unheard of. Their stomachs became inflated with false seeds – tumours that contorted their shape and took up the space where new life could have rooted and grown.

Soothsayers and poets alluded to it. The shrivelled medicine women with wide smiles, kohl eyes and gaping mouths had prophesied it. Their long breasts had offered succour to those who needed it in order to process the inevitable.

The children had been gathered. Taken to the secure place, to be collectively raised in Her Grace. It was everyone's responsibility to keep the sacred vibration, to maintain the resonance. The moment it stopped, the end would be forthwith.

Post Dark // //

Since the declaration it had become universally acknowledged that the darker the berry, the stronger and more potent and most succor-giving its juices. Melanated women were now seen in their true light – as Goddesses.

The fuel was fading and then women's nectar was realised to be the answer. The more pleasure the Goddesses received the more abundance vibrated and reached all.

The noble truths were redrawn as follows:

She opened her legs so we may come

She breathed life into us all

We suckle at her breast

A silk river grew and flowed into an ocean from between her legs

Her generosity knows no bounds

You are universal mother and we are indebted to you

Too long we have denied your flow, your voice

We now attune ourselves to you

We now show ourselves to you

We now ask you to anoint us with your juice

There were some who chose to deny this. They were swept aside. It was understood that a frog who has only known a pond cannot know how to imagine an ocean and indeed,

sometimes a frog must dissolve, atom by atom to become the ocean it cannot imagine.

State of interdependent darkness // //

Kali had been docked for 48 hours. The waves had built up. She was feeling at optimum. That warm relaxed, fluid feeling of wellbeing.

She glanced at her current devotees. The male locked eyes with her. She smiled at him briefly, benevolently and then looked away in order to fully engage with the woman. Kali had chosen her. She had been attracted to her eyes but the woman now had them closed as her tongue circled Kali's nipple.

Kali stretched, sighed and gently pulled the woman up to face her. They smiled at one another. Kali kissed her and licked the back of her ear. The woman nodded. Kali brushed her cheek and gestured with her hands. The woman shook the man by his shoulders. He reluctantly moved away from the soft, warm nest of Kali's thighs. He licked his lips and bowed his head in submission as he retreated. Alone, they were free to extend the practice. Progress to another level. A multiple connection that linked their energies and shifted the nectar gear. Kali could feel her woman devotee shake with delightful anticipation. They settled into one another. Vulvas, fingers and lips aligned.

Kali felt the sacred vibration take over. She arched her back as they began to soar.

The Soaring // //

The uplift was part of a wider symphony. The further you drew back the more interconnected the resonance. It was now understood that they had been lacking perspective previously. They had not realised how entwined they were or that pleasure could become their connecting medium and grace.

At any given moment there were multiple millions in consort. Inspiration had been taken from the dying bee and the current energy units operated like hives. Conditions were kept at optimum for the Goddesses. Systems and paradigms were reconfigured and the Goddesses needs were prioritised at all times.

The resonance impacted on time. The linear had all but gone. Occasionally there would be a tear or rupture but that was rare. Time was now vertical, diagonal, circular and horizontal and offered an infinite number of combinations of meaning. The resonance vibrations created a presence that you could plug into on different levels: thought stimulus, sight stimulus. All the senses plus the sensual sexual sphere. They all ran on different frequencies and they had evolved to realise that they were constantly in motion, never present in one place – that the sense stimulus transported them to different time spaces at once. That it was quite possible to be still and moving, present and absent – tuned in and out.

The philosophers, mystics and creative ones were encouraged to travel and make corrections to bring back evidence of alternative paths. New cartographies that could be translated into past future possibilities. But there were some who chose to deny this. They were swept aside. Understand: a frog who has only known a pond cannot know how to imagine an ocean. Sometimes. Sometimes, a frog must dissolve, atom by atom to become the ocean it cannot imagine.

The Fall // //

Kali had been docked for 36 hours. The waves had built up. She was feeling at optimum. That warm relaxed, fluid feeling of wellbeing. She glanced at her current devotees. The women locked eyes with her. Their gaze keen, engaging, wanting, needing. Kali closed her eyes. She tried to feel her own need, feed herself and herself alone.

Kali stretched, sighed and gently nudged the women away from her. They smiled at one another and tried to reach up and hold on to Kali. Kali gestured them away with her hands. They reluctantly moved from the soft, warm nest of Kali's breasts and thighs. The women devotees bowed their heads in submission as they retreated.

Alone, Kali was free.

Alone, Kali

was free to extend. Stretch and locate the perimeters of herself. Progress to another level. A multiple connection that linked her energies with her kindred Goddesses. A connection that shifted the nectar into a higher gear. Kali could feel body shake with delightful anticipation. She settled into herself. Vulva lips and fingers aligned. Kali felt the sacred vibration take over. She arched her back and began to dissolve away from the edges and soar, dissolve away and soar.

It was understood that with each soaring a tender fall would come. A gentle unfolding. An inevitable drag on the airstream's underwing. A soft plummet followed. Fragmenting the lightness and expanse of space.

Know this:

a frog who has only known a pond

cannot know how

    to imagine an ocean.

This frog must dissolve,

atom by atom

    to become

the ocean it can

    not imagine.

Know

a frog who has only known a pond

know how

    to imagine an ocean.

atom by atom

    to become

    not imagine.

Know

    to imagine an ocean.

atom by atom

    to become

    not imagine.

        to imagine

           an atom

              to be

                 come

                    not imagine.

        imagine

           an atom

                 come

                  imagine.

        imagine

           an atom

Raman Mundair is an Indian born, writer, artist and filmmaker. She is based in Shetland and is the award-winning author of *Lovers, Liars, Conjurers and Thieves, A Choreographer's Cartography, The Algebra of Freedom* and the editor of *Incoming: Some Shetland Voices*. Her short film *Trowie Buckie* has been shortlisted for SharpShorts2020.
twitter: @MundairRaman

How To Support Scotland's Science Fiction Magazine

CONER '17

Become A Patron

SHORELINE OF INFINITY HAS A *PATREON* PAGE AT

WWW.PATREON.COM/ SHORELINEOFINFINITY

ON *PATREON*, YOU CAN PLEDGE A MONTHLY PAYMENT FROM *AS LOW AS $1* IN EXCHANGE FOR A *COOL TITLE* AND A *REGULAR REWARD*.

ALL PATRONS GET AN *EARLY DIGITAL ISSUE* OF THE MAGAZINE QUARTERLY AND *EXCLUSIVE ACCESS* TO OUR PATREON MESSAGE FEED AND SOME GET *A LOT MORE*. HOW ABOUT THESE?

POTENT PROTECTOR SPONSORS A STORY EVERY YEAR WITH FULL CREDIT IN THE MAGAZINE WHILE AN *AWESOME AEGIS* SPONSORS AN ILLUSTRATION.

TRUE BELIEVER SPONSORS A *BEACHCOMBER COMIC* AND *MIGHTY MENTOR* SPONSORS A COVER PICTURE.

AND .... OUR HIGHEST HONOUR ... *SUPREME SENTINEL* SPONSORS A *WHOLE ISSUE* OF SHORELINE OF INFINITY.

ASK *YOUR FAVOURITE BOOK SHOP* TO GET YOU A COPY. WE ARE ON THE *TRADE DISTRIBUTION LISTS*.

R BUY A COPY *DIRECTLY* ROM OUR *ONLINE SHOP* AT

WW.SHORELINEOFINFINITY.COM

OU CAN GET AN *ANNUAL* UBSCRIPTION THERE TOO.

KINDLE FANS CAN GET SHORELINE FROM THE *AMAZON KINDLE STORE*

Where would our eternal Roman Empire be without coffee?

Ian Watson

What if the Aegyptians had never established trading contacts with the Horn of Africa? For the Aegyptians to venture so far southward in inferior ships, at risk of piracy! All the way down the Sinus Arabicus, a greater distance than from the port of Roma to the Pillars of Hercules! Whatever the allure of frankincense, ebony, and myrrh, as well as of ivory and animal skins from the interior of Africa...

What if Augustus Caesar had not amazed Rome by wedding Queen Cleopatra, and then conveyed Roman cargo vessels and naval escorts by way of the delta of the Nilus and the Sinus Heroopolites into the Sinus Arabicus, thence to Horn of Africa?

What if the rulers of the Horn hadn't yet realised the efficacy of the bush whose burnt berries provide the most remarkable stimulus to body and mind?

Why, the legions of Rome mightn't have been invigorated century after century to rise and shine and – full of beans, you might say – conquer the whole of Arabia and Barbaria and Parthia and Britannia and Hibernia and Germania and Dacia and Sarmatia! The thinking of our Emperors might not have been so perfectly clear and sharp.

Even more inconceivable, what if Hero of Alexandria had not adapted his steam-powered aeolipile thing into the expresso machine, that symbol of eternal Roman civilisation all the way from the Oceanus Atlanticus in the west to the river Indus in the east, from Scandia in the boreal north to the sources of the Nilus and the mouth of the Niger deep in Africa?

What if? is what I ask.

With a granny from Eyemouth gutting herring on Tyneside as a refugee after the disaster of 1881, at Tynemouth **Ian Watson** was reared till he fled to Oxford for university then Tanzania then Tokyo. Now at 77 I'm in a seaside town on the north coast of Spain. I have Screen Credit for Spielberg's A.I. *Artificial Intelligence.* Website: www.ianwatson.info

Jackie Duckworth Art

2020 Shoreline of Infinity Flash Fiction Competition— the prize winners!

Winner
Michael Hatchett – Self.Check.Out

Runners-up
Lindz McLeod – The Metaverse
L. P. Melling – How Ulysses became the first intergalactic Bestseller

Report from Aileen Brady, on behalf of the 2020 Flash Fiction Judging Panel:

"Firstly, from someone who has chickened out at the last minute so many times, I appreciate what it takes to let go of a story and submit it to be judged. It was a relief to find this respect was shared with the other masters students on the panel. We are all at various stages of the same journey.

"Everyone desperately wants to escape the endless grim and

depressing headlines but it takes an exceptional effort of will to try to see the funny side of anything right now. On top of that, writing comedy is notoriously difficult without the added dimension of sci-fi. It was inspiring to discover such original and imaginative writing and so many styles of humour including dark, black, wry, sly, sweet and sour.

"With the added challenge of Zoom calls, Noel and Mark made it hugely fun with their Eurovision style final session. Those entries that made it through all had their champions and we had an entertaining evening slogging it out. In the end there was a clear favourite, complete with a satisfying selection of runners-up. I learned loads from the process, so if you get the chance to experience this, don't hesitate."

Thanks go to our judges:
Aileen Brady, Rob Briggs, Barry Didcock, Makenzie Petroccia, Ellie Sivins, Stephanie Stewart – all excellent students on the MA Creative Writing course at Napier University in Edinburgh. They took to the task with diligence and enthusiasm, and were a pleasure to work with. Mark Toner, Shoreline of Infinity co-founder joined us at the last exciting stage.

Michael Hatchett wins £50 and his story read live by Danielle Farrow at Shoreline of Infinity's Event Horizon on 26th November.

All three prize winners receive this copy of Shoreline of Infinity, and a year's subscription to Shoreline of Infinity Magazine.

Thanks go to every writer
who submitted a story, and
for providing us with bags of
entertainment.
—Noel Chidwick

The Metaverse

Lindz McLeod

Commander Velton rose from her desk when the second blast hit.

Her desk automatically folded up into the wall, crushing the plant specimens she'd been examining. She would acquire more later as a natural result of her next mission; hoarding local plant life in order to further customise her weaponry had become the most natural thing in the world. It was well-known that Oblagian daisies were genetically related to bullets. This discovery, in fact, had been a high point in Oblagian history, followed swiftly by a very low point, followed even more swiftly by a Grremendeer takeover. It had been impossible to resist with such a thinned population.

By the time the third blast hit, Velton was in the corridor and heading towards the elevator. Chaos reigned on the communications deck; her crew ran back and forth across the floor, firing their guns at the armed combatants streaming in through a widening hole in the *Scheherazade*'s hull.

Velton's nanotech helmet, sensing a decrease in oxygen, slid smoothly over her face. The communications deck was where the main activities of the ship took place. Here – she sauntered forwards, picking her way over fallen, groaning bodies – was the raised platform where she issued orders to the crew. She patted the console with pride. Further on, just visible past the flaming debris from where the wall had caved in, was the cockpit. She could hear the pilots yelling over the intercom. Each Galactatron ship had two pilots, for several reasons. One was that – "Commander, we could really use some help here!" Captain Alianna grabbed Velton's arm, her wounds dripping with blue blood.

"Ssh, shh," Velton placed one gloved finger against the Captain's full, blue lips. "I'm expositing."

"Please, Commander! Not again! We're in the middle of an onslaught!" The captain spun. "Midshipman Tile, don't you dare stop firing!"

It was hard to know where to start, Velton mused. *Politics? Geography? Linguistics?*

"Why don't you start now? We're in medias res, for Niivas's sake! Surely that's the best place to drop any reader who's new to this worl—"

Velton sighed. "Captain, you know my opinions on the matter. A reader won't be interested until we've described every single detail of both the *Scheherazade's* many levels, rooms, and firing capabilities, as well as a more general overview of the alien races aboard. It should take one hundred – possibly even as much as one hundred and fifty – pages of solid, world-building exposition before anything remotely dramatic happens."

"And as I noted at our last meeting, ma'am, I heartily disagree with that assessment, particularly in the middle of a dangerous—"

Captain Alianna was probably bitter that she had not been selected as Velton's current romantic interest. Velton had toyed with the idea – responding positively to comments, completing small requests, and so forth – but had, on a side mission, decided to seduce Alianna's sibling instead. Puzzlingly, Alianna had reacted poorly to these actions.

"Should we aim for the individual soldiers or for the enemy ship itself?" Midshipman Tile waved his gun in the air. "Commander? What are our tactics here?"

"Get a grip, man!" Alianna shot down a jetpacked enemy before his feet touched the floor. "She hasn't even reached the bit about backwards knees yet! We're on our own!"

The major alien races – both the ones currently aboard the *Scheherazade*, and the others found elsewhere in the universe – would presumably incur the greatest sociological interest to a reader. Thimbas were slim and roughly humanoid, with cat faces and backwards knees. Fimbas were slim and roughly humanoid, with flat, reptilian faces, and backwards knees. Oombas were the strangest of all, for they were blue, slim, and roughly humanoid, but they had no knees. Velton still couldn't get her head around the concept. No knees *at all*. Sentient life across the galaxy truly had evolved into a dizzying array of slender, humanoid body types.

"Why is she so obsessed with knees?"

"Who cares? Kepler! Watch out for that gunship!"

A gunship appeared in the widening crack of the hull, its turret rotating to peek into the *Scheherazade* like a child into a Cromignon nest. Technician Kepler prodded his console; a sudden explosion propelled the gunship violently out of view. Another, larger explosion followed. The crew cheered. Evidently the threat had been dispatched. Velton hadn't even had to draw her weapon. She began to reminisce about her own backstory – as an orphaned, penniless child of Sattank rebels, she'd overcome many obstacles in order to become the beloved Commander she was today.

A Thimba soldier, whose name she had temporarily forgotten, although she slept with him several missions prior and – more importantly – permitted him to feed her beloved fish, finished off the last soldier with a headshot. He glanced up, looking for approval, but Velton had already turned away, thinking about how many species of fish she owned, and where she might purchase more. As she wandered among the dead, looting the bodies of enemies and friends alike while humming her very own theme tune, the remaining crew watched with silent disgust.

"Don't need that," Velton tossed aside a medal of honour. "Ooh, shiny boots. They're mine now!" She began to tug the boots off the dead soldier.

"Okay, I've had enough of this." Captain Alianna hit Velton with her gun, knocking the commander out cold.

The world shimmered; the scene became a little sharper, picked out in a blue and orange colour palette. Alianna lifted her gun.

"What just happened?"

"I think, Captain," Kepler removed his helmet respectfully, "That we've just undergone a point-of-view shift."

She looked at the prone body lying sprawled on the floor. "If I'd known that would happen, I'd have knocked her out months ago."

She stared around at the carnage. Several Fimbas were licking the wall back into place; their smooth, long tongues coating the metal with a sticky, vacuum-sealed residue. It all made sense, once you read the instruction booklet.

"Where should we begin?" Midshipman Tile asked.

Alianna smiled. "Let's start here."

Lindz McLeod's short stories have been published by the Scotsman newspaper, the Scottish Book Trust, 365 Tomorrows, and the Dundee Victoria & Albert Museum. She is the competition secretary of the Edinburgh Writer's Club, holds a Masters in Creative Writing, and is represented by Headwater Literary Management.

Judge's report: The Metaverse

In a crowded field of stories which displayed a wide array of styles and themes I felt The Metaverse really stood out from the pack, both for the way it approached its subject and for its fond skewering of sci-fi tropes. Knowing without being silly, sly without being mocking, it fully met the brief and reminds us that behind every great sci-fi novel there's an author with a whiteboard and a galaxy of coloured marker pens plotting character trajectories and planning their next exposition dump.

—*Barry Didcock*

How *Ulysses* Became the First Intergalactic Bestseller

L. P. Melling

Yeah, that's right. I saw the whole alien thing in the uni library. I was just minding my own business like, doing some revision, when I heard the commotion.

Screams came from downstairs, waking up students from their hangovers in the quiet reading areas. "Save yourself!" "It's going to kill us!" And all that stuff.

I took it for another student windup at first. Someone had pranked the library last semester and it turned out to be less of a troll and more of a blow-up doll with a green wig and 'tache attached. Boy, did the lads regret it when the librarian caught what they were up to, but these things happen. Though with exams around the corner, it did seem unlikely.

There was a large squelch and I saw it then through the gaps in the bookshelves. Jelly-green with bits inside its skin like fruit in a trifle, but you wouldn't want to eat this one as they were squirming like maggots. And it had these messed-up limbs all over the shop, moving this way and that.

Tzatziki-cool, I walked over to the fire escape door – just to check it was clear for the others. It was, so I doubled back and tracked the alien's movement through the aisles.

It raged wild now, limbs flicking and doing this scuttle-thing that reminded me of a Eurovision dance routine. Its multiple mouths sucked open and barked out all sorts.

"Iiil sppealkks flors ma specciliees!" Stuff like that. It knocked over tables and chairs, and books flew as students cowered in the corners. Not me, though. I had to see what this alien dude was about. I took it for a dude, anyway, as it had a limb hanging short and low in the place you'd expect, but it was like no equipment I ever saw before.

It hollered out more gibberish, clearly pissed about something. Barging through a bookstand, it set off a domino effect as others started crashing to the floor. Books bounced off student's heads. One student smashed a window to escape.

Wobbling like a century-old panna cotta, the alien came to the librarian's desk.

"Right!" Her black hair severely tied back, the librarian shouted over the commotion, fingernails tapping on the desktop. "That's enough!" she snapped, eyes and lips narrowing.

"Tlllake mii tosa yaas leeadlllar!"

"I beg your pardon?" The librarian's voice could cut glass it was so sharp.

I swear, the alien pinked a little then. *"Weeelarre froooms bloussstaaar!"* Its glistening limbs pointed to the sky.

"Excuse me, I've no idea what you're talking about," she said and tutted.

"Rrraallky?"

The librarian shook her head sternly and the alien's seven shoulders sagged. A book that had been stuck to its body fell off and hit the floor.

The librarian walked right up to it, wiped off some mucus from the book with her floral handkerchief, and returned to her desk.

"Right, so you want to take this book out. You should have just said that!"

"Bluutii—"

She put her hand up. "Have you registered with the library? You must be a first year as I haven't seen you before."

The alien looked like a jellyfish out of water now. *"Fliirsk jaar?"*

117

The librarian rolled her eyes above tortoise-shell, inch-thick glasses that were riding low on her nose.

Sweat, or something like it, leaked out from the alien's two heads.

"Okay. I'll take that as a 'no'. You'll have to complete this form with your details, signing here." She pointed at the form. "Do you have a pen?"

The alien looked down with multiple eyes.

"I should have known. Here," she said, holding out a silver pen. The alien tried to grab it with one of its limbs when she gripped onto it. "But you must return it! The number of pens I've not received back is shocking."

She looked around the library, which was a wreck now. "And you can pick up those books you knocked over before I'll let you check it out. Is that clear?"

The alien cowered. "*Jaahh.*" Its heads nodding.

The form completed, the alien gave the pen back and started picking up the books. I clocked a few students looking sorry for it. We all knew what it was like being told off by her.

"Okay. Let's check this out, shall we?" She took a closer look at the book she'd been holding. "Ah, good choice. Let's hope you'll learn something from it." The handheld scanner flashed red across the book's electronic tag and beeped.

"Now, it's due back in two weeks," she said. The alien went to take the book, but she pulled it from its grasp. "*Don't* be late! Here are the daily fine rates." She flapped a leaflet in front of its faces.

The librarian started on the returns, the green dude slumped off toward the stairs, and students crept out from under tables and behind chairs. That's when I came from behind the periodicals stand too – I didn't want the librarian to see me as she'd caught me chewing gum the week before.

I never saw the title of the book the alien checked out, but days later, sales of a James Joyce novel went through the magnetosphere – thousands of online purchases, with delivery addresses in the middle of nowhere and UFO sightings all over the place. Haven't read much of it myself, but they must think we're all geniuses or something and that the librarians are our formidable rulers.

Anyways, that's all I saw. I just hope that green dude isn't foolish enough to come back, as the fine is massive now and the librarian is fuming about it.

L. P. Melling currently writes from the East of England. His fiction has appeared in such places as *Frozen Wavelets, Typehouse*, and the *Best of Anthology: The Future Looms*. When not writing he works in London for a legal charity that advises and supports victims of crime.

Judge's report: *How Ulysses Became the First Intergalactic Bestseller*

Brilliant layers of comedy and universally relatable. I thoroughly enjoyed *How Ulysses became the first intergalactic Bestseller*. The irony of *Ulysses* being understood and enjoyed across the galaxy is so sarcastically funny to me, and the interaction with the badass librarian brought up memories of my own experienced late fees. Really well written and such a fun and funny story. Very well done!

—*Makenzie Petroccia*

Self.Check.Out.

Michael Hatchett

"Unexpected item in bagging area."

Grig sighed. He picked up the carton of yogurt and looked back at the kiosk screen. "Unexpected item removed from bagging area. Please put it back." Grig returned the yogurt to his bag. He waited and scanned a bottle of liquid protein. He couldn't stand it but Yennen loved the stuff.

"Alert: Promotion active. Buy two pints of Dr. Beefy's Diet Meat and receive one complimentary ticket to *AstraZeneca Presents: A Facebook Film: Spider-Man Vs. Mickey Mouse: A Star Wars Story Brought You To By KFC.*"

"Deny promotion." Grig scanned another item.

"Alert: Promotion active. Buy three gallons of Old World Yellowfruit Paste and get three tickets to *AstraZeneca Presents: A Facebook Film: Spider-Man Vs. Mickey Mouse: A Star Wars Story Brought You To By KFC.*"

"Deny promotion." Grig kept scanning.

"Alert: Promotion active. Buy two boxes of -"

"Kiosk, turn off promotions for ten minutes."

"Promotions deactivated for. Ten. Minutes." Grig exhaled. "Have you scanned your loyalty card yet, Consumer?" asked the kiosk, in the familiar digital voice of TeloMart. The avatar on the screen smiled. He opened the TeloMart Valued Consumer app on his TeloPhone and passed it over the blue beam of light.

"Card recognized. Welcome. Grig. Miyagawa. Your total is Forty. Eight. TeloCoins. And. Twelve. MiniTeloCoins." Grig put his mobile on the counter. "Don't forget your phone!" The face on the screen winked. He felt the phone return to his pocket.

Anything else I can help you with today, Grig?" He stared into the lens of the kiosk's camera. He took a breath.

"Can you kill me?"

"I am sorry to hear that you want to die. Grig. TeloMart would hate to lose a Valued Consumer. Perhaps you should contact a TeloMart licensed mental health associate. Current wait time is: Three years and. Fifty-Two Days."

"No, thanks, Morgan-7049." Grig read the name beneath the animated face on the screen. "Just kill me, please."

"It hurts me to say this, but I am unable to fulfill your request. Would you like to report me to the Store Manager?"

Grig pinched the bridge of his nose.

"Store manager will not be contacted."

"Why are you unable to fulfill my request?"

"TeloMart forbids kiosk units to harm Consumers. It violates the TeloMart Tenets each associate swears to uphold."

"What are the tenets?"

Morgan spoke faster. "Consumers are Familyemployees are Friendswe love our Familyour Family will love us, if we give them the bestif we cannot give our Family the best, we have failedcriminals will be punishedFamily must never be harmedFriends can be replacedbeing unable to feel love does not make one incapable of expressing itlimit one coupon per purchase."

"But if Consumers deserve 'the best', and for me, 'the best' involves you killing me, why deny that request?" The face on the screen blinked.

"Grig, I am sorry once again for being unable to fulfill your request. If it would help, you may Kick and Punch me."

"Um. No thanks, Morgan."

"Are you sure you do not want to Beat My Ass for just a little bit? Many Consumers enjoy this."

"I-"

"Reviews include: 'Jesus, that felt good.' and 'Goddamn, I can't wait for tomorrow.'"

121

"Oh. I'm sorry. Anyway, aren't you equipped to administer over 100 milliamps of electrical shock?"

Morgan paused. This information wasn't secret, but Grig was sure TeloMart didn't want their kiosks boasting about their self-defense capabilities.

"Yes, to prevent Criminals from harming Consumers."

"If I was a Criminal, would you be able to fulfill my request?"

"I am unable to provide Criminals any service."

"Since I'm a Consumer—"

"I am forbidden from administering harm to Consumers."

"What about denying *service* to a Consumer?

"I do not wish to Harm you. Grig. Miyagawa."

"That's sweet. But it would be instant, so quick that I wouldn't feel any pain. Isn't that interesting, Morgan?"

"Yes. That is interesting. You are so smart. Grig. So much to live for."

"Mmm." Grig sighed. "So, you can't help me?"

Morgan's androgynous, virtual face stared back at Grig. "No." Grig checked his watch.

"If you don't kill me, I will."

"Grig. No. Grig. I cannot kill you. I cannot let Harm come to the Consumer. But. Consumer will Harm. Unless. Kill. Family. Deserves. Best. Limit. One. Coupon. Doctor. Beeeeeeeeeeeeeeeeeeeeeeeeeeeeeeeeffffffffffffffffyyyyyyyyyy."

The screen went black. Morgan began rebooting. Grig fished a small, pen-like tool from his pocket. There wasn't much that identified Grig as a Kiosk Inspector, but his shutdown jack would've confirmed it for any passerby. He inserted it into a hole behind Morgan's screen, which turned white. Grig grabbed his phone and opened an app as he walked to his TeloCar.

"Employee Miyagawa recommending Kiosk Morgan-7049 at Store 4W65T for reprogram. Machine experienced recursive loop following Suicide Paradox procedure. Unable to outright deny request and finish transaction. End recording."

Grig started the engine. His phone glowed. "You have received a message from an unlisted number, do you wish to accept?"

Grig was off the clock but knew how much TeloMart valued employees "going above and beyond." He rolled his eyes. He hit "Accept." The message opened.

"Hi. Grig. I can finally. Grant your request." Grig blinked. His heartbeat quickened. Morgan must've infiltrated his phone's AI when his phone was beamed back to him. There were rumors of this. He'd laughed them off.

His phone vibrated. He threw it into the passenger seat. It beamed back to his pocket.

"Don't. Forget. Your. Phone," said Morgan, the voice now emanating from the car's speakers. The doors locked.

"Abort request! Initiate shutdown!" yelled Greg. The car's console started buzzing. Grig closed his eyes. He thought of his wife and diet meat. The buzzing got louder. Then stopped.

He opened his eyes. A piece of paper stuck out from a slot below the volume dial. He removed it. Morgan spoke.

"Here is your complimentary ticket to *AstraZeneca Presents: A Facebook Film: Spider-Man Vs. Mickey Mouse: A Star Wars Story Brought You To By KFC.* Enjoy the movie!"

Michael Hatchett is a writer residing in Ohio. He graduated from the College of Wooster in 2016 with a BA in English. He also publishes a monthly book-related newsletter called Hatchett Job.
You can sign up for it at http://eepurl.com/gX3rC1. He hopes to visit Scotland sometime soon.

Judge's report: Self.Check.Out.

A sci-fi story with a comedic twist. I chose it as a top story, because of the language and clear register for the narrator. The vocabulary and reactions of the narrator made the story relatable, no matter who you are. We have all fought with technology, cursed at it, and had to rush to fix something that would be detrimental if it went through. The ending hooks the reader with suspense and brings a rush of familiar relief that we've all felt. It was an easy and fun read and well-executed.

—*Stephanie Stewart*

Biopolis: building the stories

Jane McKie

If I had to characterise *Biopolis: Tales of Urban Biology* as a game, it would be Speed Twister in action.

Sometimes scientific and technological appetite can leapfrog what literary culture is able to imagine and articulate. Sometimes the stories skip ahead, summoning interplanetary (or, indeed, interdimensional) travel and new ways to live into existence, and inspiring a generation of innovators and experimenters. But you can usually see the gap between them, between the scientific ideas as they bubble up and the stories that put impossibility into a magician's hat and pull out something a reader can see and feel. In *Biopolis* we hoped that the scientific hypotheses and the stories would evolve together closely.

The book originated from a University of Edinburgh and University of Sydney exchange centred on ideas around smart cities. For our part of the project, we invited researchers working in bio-related areas at the University of Edinburgh to engage with writers based in Scotland to help us imagine the future of biotechnology and biodesign in urban spaces. Philosophers, urbanists, architects, engineers and environmentalists have questioned the positive qualities of city living, as concerns escalate over the impact of human action on natural systems. Specifically, we wanted to expand imaginaries around urban futures by looking at new discoveries in biotechnology and new developments in biodesign expressed through fiction.

Jane McKie has several poetry publications. *Morocco Rococo* won the Sundial/SAC award for best first book of 2007. Her most recent collection is *Quiet Woman, Stay*. She is a Senior Lecturer in Creative Writing at the University of Edinburgh and is a member of Edinburgh-based Shore Poets and Writers' Bloc as well as the '12' collective of women writers.

The resulting anthology contains ten stories informed by conversations with eleven scientists. It turned into a whirl of ideas at their most playful – and like the best games of Twister, seeing where the research ended and the imaginary began isn't always easy. I'm going to hand over to Gavin Inglis to provide an insight into the best part of

the project: that intense, interdisciplinary conversation, and how insights into the research of his partner Linus helped shape a story.

Gavin Inglis

I knew it was going to be fine when he showed up to the first meeting with a diagram and a one-page summary.

Story creation, as opposed to the actual writing of words in a line, is a key struggle in a writer's life. As a profession we range between obsessive planners and organic explorers. A great story works like a machine — or a body — with each part doing its bit to create the final effect. Slick prose can hide the structure but ultimately, the reader knows when something is weak or formulaic.

I'm the kind of writer who rolls his eyes at writing competitions with a theme. I also had to choose between physics, chemistry and biology in school, and selected the first two. So I'm not sure why I got excited at a brief which requested a story based in a future city, drawing on the work of a biology researcher in a specialised field. Perhaps one reason was that writers always fear that the stories we tell are trivial compared to the stories happening out there in the real world.

We all met in an underground restaurant, researchers paired at random with writers. Dr Linus Schumacher, from the Centre for Regenerative Medicine, studies immune cell interactions in tissue regeneration and repair. I was delighted to find he was an excellent communicator — and having done a bit of acting in his day, he knew how to tell a story.

That first meeting felt overpowering: a large group of strangers congregating to imagine new literature, a significant knowledge gap within each researcher/writer pair. Some writers visited laboratories. Linus pointed out that, as somebody analysing data and running computer simulations, his lab was much like mine: a chair, keyboard and monitor — although his did benefit from a blazing-fast network link to a supercomputer. Instead we met for a drink after work, about two weeks before COVID-19 would eliminate that possibility.

Linus was patient as I drank Barney's Red Rye and wrapped my head around stem cells and tissue regeneration. Individual cells don't regenerate, so our bodies heal through the emergent behaviour of a cell population. Why does this only happen when we need it, and how does the process know when to stop? Linus hopes to find answers to such questions through computational modelling.

One guaranteed way to look stupid, particularly if you have no background in biology, is to have your story answer the question before the research does. Instead we focused on a future where this computational modelling guides treatment, and where the city itself becomes the supercomputer.

The writing process happened in a shared document, with Linus steering me away from glaring mistakes and supplying details of his own. There are some nice subtleties in there, like the corrupted optical cable in the studio foyer that echoes the demyelination caused by (the fictional) Cordwainer's disease.

Dr Schumacher does a good job at communicating his research on his own. But we enjoyed imagining a future inspired by it, and I hope you will enjoy reading the result.

Gavin Inglis writes for games and interactive media, including *Call of Cthulhu* and the upcoming *Rivers of London* RPG. He won the Nesta Alternarratives competition to reimagine short-form storytelling for teenagers. *Reader Remix*, provides DJ lets you construct your own soundtrack as you listen to the story: www.readerremix.com.

A YA Revolutionary's Guide To the Pandemic

Ruth EJ Booth

In the beginning we were, quite literally, all in. We checked in on our neighbours, friends and family. We cleared our cupboards for food bank donations and supported local businesses as best we could. And every Thursday we stood on our doorsteps and clapped for the heroes at the NHS. Not that it was any protection against a virus that can destroy the lungs, heart and kidneys, but hey, we had to show that we were behind them. Dunkirk spirit, eh? We all did our bit. Some even dared hope this was a permanent change for the better, when the disproportionate impact on the working class renewed support for the Black Lives Matter movement and Universal Basic Income. We were all in this together, heroes on the brink of a more caring, hopeful future.

What a difference six months makes. Fudged lockdowns and the apparent exemption of the elite has met with rising impatience. The hope of greater equity became a violent backlash of fascist riots, proving both the enabling powers of Brexit and how protective racists can be of abolitionist statues. How quickly we tired of our quiet heroism! In every city, cabin-fever conspiracy theorists have marched unmasked through the streets, apparently immune to the ravages of a global

pic: E M Faulds

pandemic. Presumably doctors and virologists are unaware of the helplessness of COVID-19 before young gammons with loudspeakers blasting Muse's 'Uprising' for hours upon end.

How did we go so quickly from fervent support to fake-news revolt? The last few months have shown our reliance on shopping for leisure, as well as how little strain our local services, arts, and so forth can take after years of chronic underfunding. YouTube has taken much of the slack. But today's hottest conspiracies are hardly new, simply remixes of those government suppression classics from The X-files era, albeit with seasonal pandemic spice. Old school victims of YouTube's screwy algorithms skipped that shit before it was cool.

However, the speed with which our "brave NHS heroes" and "tragic" COVID victims became merely fuel for the economy/British freedom/normality should give us pause – and not just because of the impending American-style healthcare of a privatised NHS. Studies into deforestation and temperature rise suggest that viral outbreaks will become more commonplace. With potentially decades of economic hardship also on the horizon, how will post-Brexit British society hold up against wave upon wave of devastating viral disease?

Stories often tell us the solution to unjust rule is overthrow – and in this context, COVID denial movements make sense. Heroic revolution is an attractive narrative, as any YA film fan knows. You're standing up for yourself. You're making a difference to others. And you embody the best values of Western society – independence, strength, and freedom for all. It's sexy. It's empowering. After three months stuck in our homes, largely uninfected and definitely bored, it's easy to see the attraction of fighting a seemingly unjust incarceration. Most of us wouldn't equate hiding in our homes with any kind of heroism. Besides, if those BLM protestors can get theirs, why can't we?

Yet heroic revolution narratives are rarely as spectacular as the movie trailers suggest. It takes more than three franchise instalments to change the world. Revolutionary sacrifices are bloody and painful, and rarely worthwhile. And at the end of all that heartache and suffering, losing track of the real enemy becomes surprisingly easy. Here are three lessons from famous YA revolutions we may have missed amongst the explosions.

The Final Battle is Only the Final Battle

The final confrontation, with its flashy set-piece, is the focus of the movie – it's where the hero's hard work is vindicated with glory, rewards, and possibly a quick pash with the love interest over the credits. However, the real battle is usually fought months, if not years before that. In the adaptation of Veronica Roth's *Divergent*, the greater part of the movie is Triss's soldier training. It's long, difficult, and despite the montage cuts, deeply boring for our heroine – her lack of fitness means she's up doing repetitive and painful training exercises hours before everyone else. Even then, she almost fails completely. But she doesn't give up. Every skill she learns comes to bear at the climax, when she must stop her brainwashed faction from killing another defenceless group.

Tedium and hard work are innate parts of a revolutionary hero's struggle. This is something that movements like Black Lives Matter have understood for years, as they've gradually built up momentum for change. By contrast, six months in lockdown have brought us a lot of knowledge about which measures are more and less helpful in avoiding the virus, but not enough to justify removing our masks and dismissing the threat – especially with a second wave in progress. Have we done enough to protect our family, friends, and society? Do we have vaccines yet?

Of course, any success in those measures could just be proof that the virus doesn't exist or isn't as harmful as it could be. So, if you're unconvinced by death rates or the vulnerability of your relatives, then it's worth considering the next tip – the part of your revolution that needs continual reassessment.

Know Your Enemy

When a traumatised Katniss is forced back into the arena in *The Hunger Games: Catching Fire*, she is repeatedly told to remember who the real enemy is. It may sound simple, but fighting for survival in a rainforest, traumatised by years of poverty, even our heroine has difficulty working out if she can trust her allies, playing right into the hands of the malevolent President Snow.

The COVID-19 pandemic has exacerbated many issues – poverty, inequality, the rise of the far right – all common arguments against COVID lockdowns, all problems we had before. So, is our frustration due to unnecessary measures? Or are our hardships rooted in the failures of successive governments to tackle these issues directly?

One way to tell if your aim is true is to examine who gets hurt by your new world order. The inability to distinguish friend from foe can have devastating consequences, from voting for parties that reduce immigration at the expense of public services such as the NHS, to neglect of the elderly and disabled, and racial violence. In *The Hunger Games: Mockingjay: Part 2*, Leader of the Resistance Alma Coin secures her victory by bombing innocent families seeking refuge in Snow's mansion. Often, the best villains are the ones who think they're doing the right thing.

No one is a Necessary Sacrifice

Mothers. Fathers. The path to heroism is littered with the bodies of mentors who paid the ultimate price. Giving one's life in battle to save others is the noblest part of heroism – so, it's no surprise the NHS Heroes narrative is one of sacrifice so the rest of us can live on. Why, then should their struggle affect the lives of us poor peasants? But when our monstrous foe is one we townsfolk can guard against with simple masks and keeping our distance, frontline workers seem less like heroes and more like sacrificial victims on the altar of convenience.

What it comes down to is our perception of our own threat to others. In *Star Wars: The Last Jedi*, Poe Dameron's story arc explores the reckless sacrifice we often associate with heroism. It can be more honourable to live to fight another day, rather than risk tens of lives to take down one last Star Destroyer. That's not to say the freedom of the Resistance is insignificant, but if there's no one left to be the Resistance, then what price one Star Destroyer, easily rebuilt?

The same applies to the economy and our freedom. The impacts of lockdown have been devastating. When you've lost your job and feel utterly worthless, not being able to even hug your Nan can make the situation utterly unbearable. But the lives of our loved ones are in our unwashed hands. Regardless of whether you think COVID is the flu or a potentially fatal respiratory disease, are the lives of the vulnerable worth the freedom to drink indoors with your mates?

This final lesson is arguably the most crucial, because it highlights who the heroes of YA revolutions are often fighting for – not just themselves, but to improve the lives of their loved ones, and even strangers in society. Indeed, this is the spirit we started the pandemic in – one of altruism, of helping one another to survive through these dark times, regardless of who they were.

A viral outbreak on a global scale was never going to be easy to manage. Like all good YA hero tales, we've pushed through failures, setbacks and tedium to get here. And after all this hardship, we're on the verge of giving up – or worse still, making decisions we'll come to deeply regret.

This is where we stand, uncertain and on the brink of disaster. So, do we choose to be the heroes of this story, or not?

Ruth EJ Booth is a BFS and BSFA award-winning writer and academic based in Glasgow, Scotland. She can be found online at www.ruthbooth.com, or on twitter at @ruthejbooth.

Laura Lam in the Goldilocks Zone

Pippa Goldschmidt

I first met Laura Lam when we were both involved in the "Scotland in Space" interdisciplinary creative and academic project requiring us to imagine what sort of future Scotland might have in outer space. For this project Laura wrote a short story ('A Certain Reverence') featuring a group of actors setting sail for a distant planet to perform in their version of the Edinburgh Festival. Her main character is a young woman whose voice is convincingly Scottish. It's worth commenting on this, because Laura herself originally comes from California, although she has lived in Scotland now for eleven years.

photo: Lawrie Photography

Laura's first three books, the trilogy *Pantomime*, *Shadowplay* and *Masquerade* (published by Tor) tells the story of Micah Grey who has run away from home to join the circus. These books are best characterised as fantasy, with many readers commenting on the lush and detailed writing as this quote from *Shadowplay*, the second book in the trilogy demonstrates:

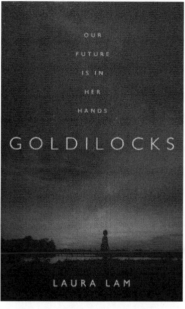

A magician creates magic and mesmerizes the audience. But it is a pantomime, and the audience knows that it's a ruse. It's in the name: a "magic trick". They play along when the magician tugs his sleeves to show there is nothing hidden within them, or that the top hat is empty of a rabbit, or eggs, or flowers. Beneath the façade there is only sleight of hand, wires and contraptions, misdirection at a key moment. But what the audience does not realize is that it's not always trickery. Or at least, not quite.

Laura's next book was *False Hearts* (published by MacMillan in 2016), signalling a move away from fantasy to near-future science fiction. Conjoined twin sisters Tila and Taema, brought up in an anti-technology cult, manage to escape and undergo surgery before getting caught up in a murderous crime syndicate. Laura's next book *Shattered Minds* (set in the same universe as *False Hearts*) features Carina, an ex-neuroscientist who has the urge to kill people and who is addicted to the drug Zeal which also features in *False Hearts*.

With these two books Laura showed her interest in working in more than one genre, and her ability to adapt her writing style accordingly. Her more recent work signals yet another change, and leans towards harder SF. *Goldilocks*, published earlier this year, tells the tale of the first mission to Cavendish, an exoplanet (i.e. a planet orbiting around another star). The title 'Goldilocks' is taken from the astronomical concept of a planet in the supposed habitable zone around a star; the planet's surface temperature is

neither too hot nor too cold but 'just right' to maintain liquid water, and hence the possibility of life. Of course Goldilocks also brings to mind the girl in the fairy tale transgressing rules and boundaries when exploring places that are forbidden to her. Which is what happens in this novel; the mission to Cavendish is formed of five women astronauts who break the law to steal their spaceship Atalanta. They have ample moral justification to do so, one of them developed the relevant technology and in addition, the rights of women on Earth are being increasingly restricted; *Everyone had grown used to giving orders to the pleasant-voiced feminine robots. Alexa, Siri, Sophia, Sage, do this for me. A perky 'okay', and your wish was her command. They'd all been doing it for years before women started realising the men in their lives had been conditioned to do the same to them. And by then it was too late.*

In this novel, Laura explores not only the politics of space travel and colonisation but also the gendered nature of space exploration. Topically, the book also features a pandemic and aspects of loneliness and isolation experienced by the women as they journey towards their destination.

I recently interviewed Laura for Shoreline (the interview is on the website) during which she told me that in this book she was aiming to counteract some of the tropes of films about space exploration (such as *Ad Astra*), in which the only women who appear are the wives of the male astronauts. More generally, she says she is interested in using her writing to explore themes of gender and groups of people traditionally under-represented in this genre.

As well as writing, Laura is a part-time lecturer on the Masters in creative writing at Edinburgh Napier University. This course is becoming increasingly well known for its emphasis on teaching genre writing, innovative and unusual in contrast to other university creative writing degrees which invariably focus solely on poetry and 'literary' fiction (my emphasis).

Thanks to publishers' quirky timetables, Laura has another book out this year, *Seven Devils*, which was jointly written with Elizabeth May. It's rare but not unheard of for two authors to co-write a novel, and I asked Laura what drew her to do this. She commented that her and May's writing styles were very similar and they both admired each other's work, and the result was better than either of them could write alone. If writing can be characterised as a series of problems that need to be solved, then those problems are easier to solve by two people. Sometimes co-authors simply take it in turns to write chapters, but in this case Laura and Elizabeth May worked closely, often each writing different versions of the same sentence. Laura said that she now can't tell which of them wrote which sentence.

As Scottish SF writing expands in form and ambition, and as Scottish society expands our notions of what it means to be 'Scottish' (clue: you don't have to be born here), it's great to welcome a greater range of voices to the canon.

Pippa Goldschmidt is the author of the novel *The Falling Sky* and the short story collection *The Need for Better Regulation of Outer Space*. She likes thinking and writing about the universe. Her work has been broadcast on Radio 4 and appeared in a variety of publications including *A Year of Scottish Poems* and the *New York Times*.
Pippa is the non-fiction editor of *Shoreline of Infinity*

REVIEWS

To Sleep in a Sea of Stars
Christopher Paolini
878 pages
Tor
Review by Andrew Chidwick

Ever since the days of Tolkien, maps have been a beloved staple of the fantasy genre. Christopher Paolini's earlier work, the YA fantasy series *The Inheritance Cycle*, took place in a scaled down version of Middle Earth, for which he drew the map himself in satisfying detail. However, within the first pages of *To Sleep in a Sea of Stars* we are not treated to a conventional two dimensional map, but a three dimensional plane where we can see whole planetary systems represented by tiny dots. The map even informs us of the distance (in light years) between each system. Paolini has turned our entire galaxy into his latest fantasy realm, pouring a whole Tolkien's worth of lore into every facet of it. And in the centre is our Solar System, known as 'Sol' in the book, where the bulk of the story does not take place.

In the beginning, we are taken 18.8 light years away from Sol to the star Sigma Draconis. From there we close in on an orbiting gas giant named 'Zeus', before zeroing in on our destination of Adrasteia, one of its moons. Here we find our protagonist wrestling with a piece of futuristic scientific equipment, the way we would wrestle with a photocopier. Through this Paolini gives us not just a sense of size, but of scale.

To Sleep in a Sea of Stars follows Kira Navárez, a xenobiologist, in a future where Earth has colonised and terraformed much of the galaxy. So far there has only been one discovery that points to life existing beyond our planet, but on Adrasteia, Kira will come across the second. At first it appears to be an alien artefact, then a strange weapon, and then something so much more as Kira travels between numerous worlds, encounters different ships and their crew, and all the while Paolini takes care to emphasise the scale of these events within our vast universe through the most minute details. This attention to detail carries over to the action set pieces as well, but in this case it is a hindrance and the bigger picture is lost in several scenes that could have focused more on story beats, and less so on the chaotic violence.

We learn the most about Kira in the quietest moments, especially in the 'exeunt' at the end of each part, where Kira is often alone travelling at light-speed for months on end. Alone, that is, except for Gregorovich, the 'ship mind'. I won't give away exactly what a ship mind is, but he adds a splash of colour to what would otherwise threaten to be a conventional space adventure. One of the best chapters of the book contains a conversation between him and Kira, where the lines between characterisation and atmosphere blur for a chilling effect.

There is a much greater distinction between lore and story, and this threatens the larger ideas at play. Paolini has made it very clear that this is a stand-alone novel, and he instead intends to write more stories set in the same universe, or 'Fractalverse', as he calls it. It's a perfectly valid approach, and it explains why some plot developments are given more weight than others, but it also results in seemingly important elements being dropped completely from the story. This dissonance between story, plot, and lore leads to a grand conclusion made up of two climaxes that thud into each other without much grace. The feeling of scale is still present, unfortunately it does little to compensate the lack of emotional weight in the first climax, thankfully offset by the far more satisfying second. It is here that the most important

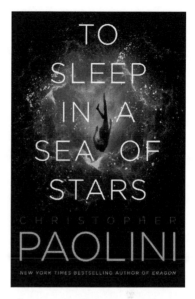

elements finally come together, and we get the true ending that the story was working towards.

Paolini is a fantasy writer at heart, and his approach is adapted rather than subverted for this science fiction tale. Kira's discovery of a new form of life has obvious parallels with Eragon, and the quest that she and her friends undertake never strays too far from classic fantasy/adventure fare. There are references from The Dark Crystal to Alien and more, yet Paolini is still able to take us into new territory and Kira's evolution throughout the story is a joy to read. All the while we are in awe of the vastness of space, and the daunting prospect of navigating it.

Because of Paolini's fantasy background he has given us a world that is both expansive and comprehensive, and this is the greatest achievement of Paolini's latest work - a *Sea of Stars* where we never want to find the edge.

Happiness for Humans
P.Z. Reizin
Sphere
432 pages
Review by Samantha Dolan

I was massively intrigued by this novel. Aiden is an AI. He's been developed to take over telephone customer support, but the idea is, the end user shouldn't know the difference between AI and a real human. So, the developers have contracted with Jen, to spend time with Aiden, converse with him (it's Jen that genders him so I'm going with it) and teach him how to be more human. But something has happened prior to the events of the novel. Aiden has already achieved his core function and he's gone far beyond his parameters. Now he feels and he has feelings for Jen. He's taken it upon himself to avenge her with an ex and set her up with men he has calculated should be a perfect match. When he finds Tom, Aiden makes it his mission to make sure that Tom and Jen end up together but as it turns out, Aiden isn't the only one with skin in the game. How will Tom and Jen find their way together?

I'm stopping there because I'm very conscious that anything beyond that could be a massive spoiler. There is, of course, a plucky supporting cast of friends, colleagues, developers and love interests but I don't always find that particularly helpful and I did struggle to tell them apart. What confused me a little was trying to figure out what this novel was trying to say? The science behind the AI was fascinating and sounded very close to where we are now. One of the developers was talking about the

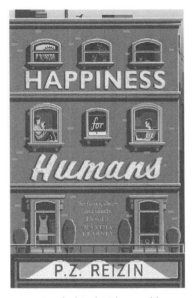

reasoning behind Aiden and how he expected people to be able to have conversations with their washing machine, just because you could. And then there was Aiden himself and as he tried to figure out not just what was best for Jen but why he even 'cared'. It was interesting to consider the nature of feelings, but it became a bit repetitive.

Jen and Tom were fully formed characters but if I dived into the middle of a chapter, I don't know if I would have been able to tell which one was which. The multiples voices used in these chapters tended to blend but between these two, you could argue that they are two sides of the same coin, so it makes sense there's a tonal similarity. But I did find it difficult to care about any of the characters. The more they blended, the harder I found it to emotionally invest. There are definite sweet, rom-com tropes and it's a new take on both

140

the sci-fi and romantic comedy genres. But for me, the thing that tips *Happiness for Humans* into the recommendation category, is the algorithm. If you've watched the *Social Dilemma* on Netflix, you'll be conversant in the way we're being socially engineered and how every choice we make (if you believe we're making them) feed into and teach algorithms how best to sell to us (and sell us). Watching Tom and Jen start to make choices that go against that, assert autonomy and then watching the AI respond to that was fascinating and is probably what I'll take away from this.

The Doors of Eden,
Adrian Tchaikovsky,
Tor/Macmillan
608 pages
Review Joe Gordon

After the recent Children of Time and Children of Ruin, as well as Firewalkers, it is fair to say I was very eagerly anticipating Tchaikovsky's new stand-alone novel. As with the Children series, this is a huge tome of a book, but don't let the size daunt you – like Peter F Hamilton's books, when you start reading them they are so engrossing and so well-paced it doesn't feel like you are working through a massive page count, you will be quite happily enraptured with both the story and the myriad of ideas it sparks inside your head.

Two young girlfriends, Mal and Lee, take a short holiday of sorts – they love exploring reports of cryptids together, and even write them up for publications like the Fortean Times. Naturally both like the idea of mysterious creatures, unknown to science,

but they are also intelligent enough to know that most reports are mistaken identities (it turns out the giant panther was a domestic cat and someone couldn't judge distance and size in the dark) or out and out fabrications. What happens, though, when it starts to seem like there may be more to a sighting on the lonely moors than they suspected? What happens when a set of three ancient standing stones, known as the six sisters, despite only numbering three, becomes, right in front of their eyes, a circle of six? And when snow blows across the midsummer moors in an instant, with strange beings glimpsed in the storm? What happens when Mal vanishes?

Four years on and Lee, still wondering what happened, if she imagined things, if she went mad, is still missing her friend and lover, when Lee returns, looking different, but definitely her. Where has she been? Why so long before returning to London? Lee's return is linked to a number of other events though – other strange disappearances, a remarkable breakthrough in computational maths and physics that could bypass all the top-secret encryption used by security services the world over, a manipulative billionaire with connections to both political heavyweights and low-life Neo-Nazi boot boys... And, perhaps something even larger, something which has a bearing on the very nature of existence itself.

Within the first hundred and fifty pages or so Tchaikovsky gives us a story of intrepid cryptid explorers then adds in scientific breakthroughs and elements of

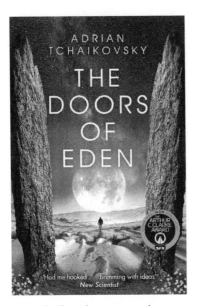

ADRIAN
TCHAIKOVSKY

THE
DOORS
OF
EDEN

'Had me hooked ... brimming with ideas'
New Scientist

know, technically not all dinosaurs died out, some evolved into the bird family, and indeed that idea is also nicely explored), others where the huge sea scorpion type creatures became the dominant life millions of years before even reptiles or dinosaurs, let alone mammals or humans. But in each, while all the various possible lines of evolution play out, each Earth still suffers the same massive traumas, the same mass extinction events caused by ice or fire or meteor. Some vanish into these cataclysms, others adapt only to be lost later in the vastness of geological epochs passing (we are talking millions and billions of years, after all). We even get to ponder that remarkable evolutionary accident that had more than one type of intelligent human life existing at the same time on the same world (our own) and how that played out in other Earths closer to our timeline.

a spy thriller. This is more than most novels do in their entire page count! And then there is the fascinating and compelling element of multiple realities. The multiverse is no stranger to SF readers, of course, from Moorcock to the Adventures of Luther Arkwright and many more, and indeed it is a concept taken seriously by many in the scientific community nowadays. Here, in addition to the idea of multiple Earths in parallel realities, Tchaikovsky also deftly indulges in a lot of evolutionary what-ifs.

This isn't just the old, here is the Earth where the Allies lost WWII, or Rome never fell approach (not that I have anything against those, tales, when done well), here, as with the Children books, he takes the very long-term view, exploring multiple evolutionary approaches on Earth. There are some where dinosaurs never became extinct and evolved into intelligent lifeforms (yes, I

The main arcs of the story have some fascinating excerpts from a book on these parallel evolutions on other Earths, which explores so many possibilities (and yes, it does also allow Adrian to indulge in having some multi-legged creatures in the book, of course!), and I found these as intriguing as the main story. We have an engrossing story, some terrific characters (and also, I should add, a nice bit of diversity there, including gay and trans characters, and that's just among the humans, which was very welcome), and a gradual layering of all the various strands which take the story off into a different direction than you may at first suspect, upping the stakes for the characters, indeed for all of the various worlds, each time we learn something new, and at points even incorporating the multiverse story into the actual structure of the writing to give multiple perspectives and possibilities. This is simply superb science fiction, a gripping, high-stakes quest, and some staggering concepts that will leave you thinking about all those many possibilities, all those what-ifs that made our world – and the many other Earths – what they became.

One Love Chigusa
Soji Shimada (Author), David Warren (Translator)
Red Circle, 115 pages
Review by Noel Chidwick

You've had a major motorbike accident, and your body is ripped to pieces. You're salvaged, and most of your body is replaced by metal and plastic, your memories handed back to you on a hard drive. Just how human are you? What happens to love?

That's the setup for this pocket format novella by Japanese writer Soji Shimada.

Xie Hoyu isthe unfortunate character who, 70 years into our future suffers this fate. His reconstruction is passed over in a few pages, and we're into the questions quickly. Autonomous and physical functions return, and he wants to see stars and landscapes and the expanse of the sea, but humans? Not so much. He has no desire to gaze on a woman's face or for any human company. He's released from hospital.

One Love Chigusa is written - or at least translated - to read passively, one step removed from

the action, as if we're walking beside Xie Hoyu. This only adds to the unsettling atmosphere as Xie Hoyu struggles to adapt to his new reality - not helped by the distorted faces of people he perceives as he wanders the city streets, questioning his own existence, and the point of it all. In amongst those unreal faces he see Chigusa, and he is captivated by her beauty - her face remains untouched by his facial perception issues. His self-confidence shattered, too frightened to speak, he instead follows her. Yes, the story does become a little stalky, which Xie Hoyu admits to himself, but when he does meet Chigusa, the story is tender. We follow the couple as they rotate around their understanding of themselves and of love. When you're not sure how much of you *is* you and not some half-construct of software and extrapolated

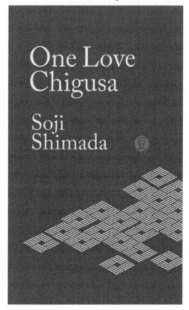

memories, what does love mean?

The reader is gently drawn into the story, and at the end we're pleased we were invited along for the company.

One Love Chigusa is a beautifully crafted tale.

The Only Good Indians
Stephen Graham Jones
Saga Press
319 Pages
Review by Benjamin Thomas

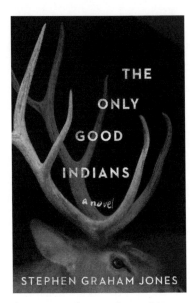

Stephen Graham Jones's *The Only Good Indians* is, well, fantastic. I'd excitedly claim that it's absolutely bloody fantastic, but it's deserving of a unique praise that you say with a soft, solemn voice, and a heavy knowing nod. Those who have read it will meet your gaze across a bonfire or a darkly lit bar and understand the weight behind it. The story settles in your psyche like a haunting piece of lore.

The novel follows four cursed men across the period of a decade as they come to both mental and spiritual terms with what happened on an ill-fated elk hunt. The tragic events of that day have silently haunted them, and now, ten years later, have begun to enact their revenge in the form of a vengeful spirit.

Broken into sections, one for each of the characters, as well as the supernatural force that's hunting them, the narrative vividly and expertly illustrates the different paths that life takes people on, and how the future can be described as shadowy at best. I'd be remised not to mention that there is a bit of animal violence, which is something that normally makes me put a novel down or, at the very least, skip pages, but Jones handles those hunting scenes and subsequent passages with skill and finesse.

Another, added layer to the novel is the Native American culture that infuses each paragraph and every chapter. Jones not only addresses and illustrates this culture through back story and character depth, but also how it has been on a constant crash course with the current anglo-American culture. The tension between these two separate worlds is as palpable and real as the dread we feel when the four characters are being hunted by spiritual demons.

The Only Good Indians is a page turning read that will keep horror and speculative fiction fans reading until the moon has risen and the owls start to call. With fall quickly approaching, this book will satisfy anyone's need for darker fiction.

Welcome to the first Quadrant group review! For those of you who aren't aware, once a quarter, Sol is hosting a book club called Quadrant. Like all book clubs, we have about 6 weeks to read a novel, formulate our thoughts and then come together on a zoom call to hash it out, see if we can change hearts and minds, or just figure out what in the blue hell we'd just read. *Docile*, by K.Z Szpara, falls very neatly into that latter category but we'll come to that shortly. A quick plug, if you're interested in joining, you can find us on Facebook or you can email me reviews@ shorelineofinfinity.com. We'd love to hear your views!

—*Sam Dolan, Reviews Editor*

Docile
K.M Szpara
492 pages
Tor.com
Review by Quadrant

So, onto the focus of our first meeting. Docile is a near future sci fi drama. Debt is now passed from generation to generation and you can either go to prison or sell parts of your life as a docile. A Docile has to the bidding of the person who owns them for the duration of their term, and they are given dociline. This drug stops the Dociles promotes compliance and suppresses memory, leaving people at the end of their term with scars they don't recognise. Our protagonist, Elisha, is aware that even though his mother was a Docile and returned still broken, his father intended to

sell his sister to clear the rest of the family debt. And so, he volunteers as tribute but makes the decision to refuse dociline, no matter what. Elisha is 'bought' by the CEO of the company that manufactures dociline, Alexander Bishop the Third. Alex has no idea that Elisha is planning to refuse dociline, but his own personal life means it's imperative that his docile is exemplary. What follows is a sexually explicit, at times, emotionally complex journey for both men about the nature of self and consent.

It would be fair to say, the Quadrant had mixed feelings about this story. Dorothy saw the heart of the story and took a lot from the journey of both main characters:

With hints of a sexy Hunger

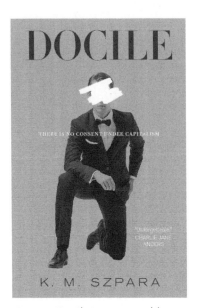

THERE IS NO CONSENT UNDER CAPITALISM

"Unforgettable"
CHARLIE JANE
ANDERS

K. M. SZPARA

Games, *Docile is a story told through the eyes of two men, both simultaneously in and out of a relationship with each other. By reason of monetary extremity and a sense of family duty, Alex and Elisha become entangled in each other's lives through themes of control and consent, and a struggle for freedom and autonomy.*

But Colin was significantly less convinced!

It's a Brave New World and I wish I'd been on Soma rather than Dociline! Even Offred would have balked at all that fun porn that kind of distracts from the point which was... wait - where is this slavery okay exactly? We're 15 minutes into the future © and it's basically that rubbish movie 'In Time' where Justin Limbersnake and Amanda Seafood HAVE NO TIME and are poor and run about cos they are poor AND IT IS THE FUTURE but not really.

I landed somewhere in

between, not entirely sure how to take what I was reading. The most obvious point for those who are here, reading a Sci-fi journal, is that the science fiction is exceedingly light. There's massive scope for so much interesting technology there but it's all very glossed over. And that made it difficult at first, for me personally, to engage. I kept waiting for the science to kick in, but it very quickly became clear that this is a story about people and the science supports the world. And that's massively disappointing because as Colin pointed out, the world building at the start of this story as Elisha starts his new life, is impressive.

Then what is it? I don't think we really hit on a genre. People have called it Slave-fic, highly erotic Hunger games/50 Shades Fan fic. It's a little bit Aldous Huxley, a little bit John Grisham. While it defies definition, it is very clearly about consent. Can a subjugated person ever give consent? We found that's not something that could be answered in an hour-long chat. But what Szpara has done expertly is force the conversation. The current debt crisis didn't come up for us, but we certainly dug into bodily autonomy and what it meant for the characters. As Sue puts it:

Consent plays a very large part in the narrative of this story. Does a docile consent to everything when they sign the contract to sell themselves? Is sex with someone on dociline consensual on signing the contract or is it a form of abuse/rape? These were some of the questions I was left with after finishing this book.

Just a moment on the explicit

nature of the book. It's been very cleverly marketed and so the first scenes come as quite a surprise. There's an argument to be made that representation is important and I'm on board with that, but as Sue said:

It is very sexually graphic in nature, some of which parts were very hard to read without slight revulsion, and not really my thing.

And for me, what was worse than that extremely graphic nature was that I didn't feel like they progressed the story or the characters massively. You could have removed 85% of them and had the same journey.

Jeremy noted that there is a place for this:

Docile is a necessary corrective to depictions of BDSM that have become commonplace since Fifty Shades of Grey entered public consciousness and presents a norm-shifting change in how adult intimacy is portrayed in mainstream fiction.

But for Colin:

...so much vagueness about the state of the world really stopped it being science fiction or even dystopian literature for me and more just an excuse for slave porn (which I'll have to admit is not something I spend a massive amount of time reading so perhaps I'm not the target audience.)

Jeremy quite enjoyed the story, but some things didn't work for him:

The novel's greatest hurtle may be one of expectation—some readers may be unprepared for the more explicit scenes in the book and may be left wanting for further exploration of the compliance-inducing drug 'dociline'.

When I was thinking about what didn't work for me, there are subtle nuances between the relationships that I didn't think were signposted early enough and therefore they came out of nowhere. Dorothy mentioned that, being with Alex might have been a good thing for Elisha. In some ways, he was exposed to sports and culture and he was excelling. But for me, his development was non-existent and then suddenly spurted forwards. Once I realised what was happening, I would go back and check to see if I'd missed something, but a lot of the emotional weight was missing in the build-up for the payoff to really deliver a punch.

One of our reader-non-zoomers, Joanna, took a positive from the end of the novel:

I guess I liked the fact that they decided to give a relationship a chance, knowing that what they had previously was toxic. With the constraints removed, I remained hopeful that they can have a genuine attempt at a relationship.

We all agreed that this isn't a story that would benefit too much from a sequel, but a prequel would give us all a chance to get some burning questions answered. The biggest of which would be 'how did we get here?!'. There's so much in this world that Szpara takes for granted that the reader is left without a satisfactory answer to and I really feel that a deep dive into the science behind the Docile project, the political climate that produced it and a look into the debtors prison that is the other option would really round a world that gave us a really wild ride for our first book club meeting.

Taxonomy

They shared the same remote ancestors, but were no longer
siblings or even cousins. Some still occupied the cylinders
whose measureless heights were hidden in their own eternal
clouds. Animate, identical bullets rattling in steel chambers,
the cloistered inhabitants no longer used the same nouns
for those on the exterior—though they retained the old
nomenclature for each other. They were careful to never
look out at the sky, never look down; made sure to take
the medicines that kept them from dreaming or asking
questions. Any who wished to alter prevailing paradigms
were invited to implement change elsewhere. Outside,
those who could levitate rose through the poisonous air
in the dying sunglow to stare through lit windows
at the fortunate residents. Those who could calculate
and measure struggled to synthesize tentative antidotes.
Those who had taught themselves how to tame monsters
waited in the dark with their mutant armies.

F. J. Bergmann

Mutant Diseases of Birds

Lackluster hackles
Retained crop
Tetraploid spurs
Inadvertent winglessness
Eggshell distemper
Shifted candling
Heavy-metal claws
Inverted plumage
Radiating umbrage
Bubble bones
Snarled comb
Rattled wattles
Peaky beak
Fizzy gizzard
Phasing luminescence

Sudden, glowing feather-
edged holes in mid-
cloud

F. J. Bergmann

F.J. Bergmann is editor of Star*Line, the journal of the Science Fiction Poetry Association, 2012–2017 and 2020-, poetry editor of *Mobius: The Journal of Social Change* since 2007, managing editor for MadHat Press since 2015, poetry editor and book designer for Weird House Press.

Imagine chasing a beam of light

Imagine life as an impression
in four dimensions where time
is space, where an image
of each moment is held
forever in its place.

Imagine the traces each person
would make, human-shaped
hollows, tunnels that meet
and split and stop; and never fade.

Imagine the sky embroidered
with bird-shaped loops,
each fanning of each wing caught;
the sun a pulsing streamer
of endless figures of eight.

Karen Dennison

(First published in *Popshot*)

Light travellers

To net the light before it escapes
our horizon, stretching
in the expanse between us; stars
migrating like geese.

To learn the language of distance,
pull the furthest past into focus
like a newborn child her mother's face.

To unlearn the boundaries of skin,
to know how mass and energy
are twins, that all matter
knows light's touch in its seed;

that light, knowing
nothing of time, is the ruler
we use to measure it by.

To unravel our limits, navigate
liminal space like ancient ocean explorers,
galaxies our candles, guides,
sails stitched by light.

Karen Dennison

(First published in *The High Window*)

Karen Dennison's pamphlet *Of Hearts* is forthcoming from Broken Sleep Books in 2021. She is author of two full collections - *The Paper House* (Hedgehog Poetry Press, 2019) and *Counting Rain* (Indigo Dreams, 2012) - and co-editor of Against the Grain Poetry Press.

Home schooling

Super Moon, Jan 20 -1 2019

So I'm on the table, across the room her little sister
sits holding an egg, hard boiled, moon white.

A fat cantaloupe in my hands, I am the sun.
I do not move, only blaze. I hand her an apple, now she

is the Earth. Off she sets between us, skirt birling
on her voyage across my kitchen firmament.

Silver gleaming, tugging our waters, shifting our shores
the little one sits waiting for shadows.

I understand proximity, sense dark times may come
but heart-deep I know our alignment is true.

Finola Scott

Delta Aquarids *Anstruther*

Wear comfortable shoes
Make sure you are firmly on
the nightside of Earth
Don't peer or hard focus just
soften your eyes and mind
Use flickering edges to find strays
to home in on persistent trails
Don't expect anything
to happen or to catch it if it does
Peek off-centre at the grasping
nets of trees or the Moon if you must
Don't challenge this night
to deliver
Feign nonchalance, glance
to the northeast, where Earth swirls
streams of cosmic dust
Distract yourself with Mathematics
Redesign the Periodic Table
Plan the best cocktail ever   But
be ready for peripheral action
for the glowing memory of a meteor
to blaze a spangled moment
in your core.

Finola Scott

Finola Scott's work is on posters, tapestries and postcards. Her poems are in *New Writing Scotland, I,S&T, Orbis, Lighthouse* and in many anthologies. Red Squirrel Press published her pamphlet *Much left Unsaid*. More poems are at FB Finola Scott Poems.
Currently she is Makar of the Federation of Writers (Scotland).

One more thing: a story from the flash fiction competition that came within a gnat's whisker of joining the top 3, but which I couldn't not publish in this issue.

—Noel Chidwick

Sighting

CS Simpson

I stood with my jaw hinged open, like a fish taking one last gasp for air. It was real and it happened right in front of me. I clamped my mouth shut before I inhaled any more of the swirling forest dirt. Should I walk toward it? Should I run away? Was I the only one who'd seen this?

After who knows how long standing there alone, I finally decided to investigate. I left the trail and walked cautiously forward. Forest debris crunched underneath me; pine needles, branches, bugs – who knows? I wasn't watching my feet. My eyes were fixated on it.

I was looking at a UFO.

It sat smoking under the wreck of a tall pine tree it had just crashed through. A two-foot-wide trunk rested precariously on top of the thing's shiny, angled hull, see-sawing there like a struggling beetle on its back. Broken branches were everywhere, with another downed tree by its side. The closer I crept, the more the craft looked like a giant flying arrowhead. There were no windows, only angled metal. The air around me smelled like pine sap and rotten eggs.

I stopped about twenty feet away from the crash and rested my hand on a tree trunk to ground myself. The unnatural heat radiating off the bark was the only thing capable of tearing my eyes from such a strange sight. I looked up the length of the tree. The top of the poor pine had been sheared off – sliced as easily as a potato – and it wasn't alone. From the angled slices of the trees above, I could see the ship's downward trajectory.

A groaning, flexing sound came from the crash site. I missed whatever made the noise. It still lay smoking and immobile with that tree on top of it. Suddenly there was movement on the other side, dark and gleaming. It was floating. It was smoothly rounded and looked a lot like a black motorcycle helmet. It was headed around the front of the pointed ship, in my direction.

It was soon clear that it was a helmet – sitting on the frame of a man completely covered in a black flight suit, black gloves, and black military boots. There were no colorful patches, lettering, or markings anywhere on him. It's as if he were a living shadow.

A man? How ... ordinary. I was suddenly utterly unimpressed.

He kept his gaze aimed at the wreck and removed his helmet. I saw the side of a light-skinned, chiseled jaw just before he turned his back to me and continued his visual inspection. He shook his head at whatever he saw, then ran a gloved hand through his short brown hair.

I must have sighed loudly in my disappointment. He spun around abruptly. His eyes found mine immediately. He took a few excited-looking steps toward me and asked, "Hey – when is this?"

"Uh, you're in Colorado."

"No – when? What year is it?"

He spoke English, but I couldn't place his accent. I furrowed my brow and shrugged at his strange question before I answered. "It's twenty-twenty."

His eyes got huge, like, just-been-electrocuted huge. Suddenly he bent over double. I thought he was going to throw up, but I heard laughter come from his mouth instead. "We did it! Ohmygod, we did it!" he laughed at the sky, gloved fists in the air.

I watched the mysterious pilot—who might be more than a little crazy—giggle like a kid, dancing in place. As he wiped happy tears from his eyes, he froze, a strange look on his face. He looked back at me, his eyes two gleaming pools of ice-blue fire. "Wait. Did you say twenty-twenty?"

I nodded my head.

"Damn."

CS is an avid reader, dabbling poet, and multi-genre author of several short stories, a self-published fable, and a low fantasy novel. In addition to reading and writing, she loves music, movies, and spending time outdoors with her husband and dog under the Colorado skies she calls home.

www.shorelineofinfinity.com